Incognita

Incognita

or

Love and Duty Reconciled

William Congreve

ET REMOTISSIMA PROPE

100 PAGES

100 PAGES
Published by Hesperus Press Limited
4 Rickett Street, London SW6 1RU
www.hesperuspress.com

First published 1692
First published by Hesperus Press Limited, 2003

Designed and typeset by Fraser Muggeridge
Printed in the United Arab Emirates by Oriental Press

ISBN: 1-84391-069-1

CONTENTS

FOREWORD

Congreve was nothing if not precocious. His first comedy appeared on the London stage in 1693, when he was twenty-two years of age, and he managed to stop writing drama altogether when he was only thirty. It is seldom that a literary reputation has been established in so short a period.

Congreve was born in Leeds, but his father's military career brought him to Ireland. He was enrolled as a pupil at Kilkenny College, where he met Swift, and then as an undergraduate at Trinity College, Dublin; in these refined surroundings he wrote *Incognita*, which smacks a little of university wit, and brought the manuscript with him on his return to England. He entered the Middle Temple in London, an institution which was then characterised by its appetite for literature rather than for law; here he wrote a play, *The Old Bachelor*, and made a rapid entry into coffee-house society. He formed an acquaintance with John Dryden, who saw the merit of his work and helped to advance his career. The revered poet undertook the revision of the young man's play, and was almost as pleased by its success as Congreve himself.

The Old Bachelor was followed by such dramas as *The Double Dealer* and *The Way of the World*, but Congreve himself, dismissing his literary endeavours as 'trifles' in later life, entered the world of government sinecures and disappeared from view. As the Victorian littérateur Edmund Gosse put it, 'He passes through the literary life of his time as if in felt slippers, noiseless, unupbraiding, without personal adventures'.

In the year *Incognita* was published, 1692, he was not so retiring. In the middle of the eighteenth century, *Biographia Britannica* proclaimed that 'he aimed at perfection from the very beginning, and his design, in writing this novel, was to show how novels ought to be written'. It has been suggested that he actually completed it in his first year at Trinity College, when he was no more than seventeen, in which case it is a truly surprising document. If it is not 'perfection' in itself, *Incognita* is perfect of its kind. It was written at the very dawn of serious fiction in England and in Europe, when the great examples were Aphra Behn and Madeleine de Scudéry. In his preface to the novel, Congreve describes it as a 'laborious idleness', no more than an 'essay begun and finished in the idler hours of a fortnight's time'. But he protests too much; it is a very accomplished performance, designed to display Congreve's not inconsiderable skills as a narrator and a stylist. The fact that it went through four editions in his lifetime suggests that its merits were well recognised from the beginning.

The plot is not its most interesting aspect. It concerns the amatory adventures of two intimate friends, Aurelian and Hippolito, who go through a series of ever smaller hoops in order to obtain the objects of their twinned desires. The scene is set in Florence, the home of Italian romance for every reader of English fiction, and the first principal 'set piece' of the narrative occurs at a masked ball in which all the main protagonists are concealed from each other. The confusions and mistaken identities of the subsequent story need not be outlined here, in the expectation that they will soon become familiar to anyone who reads the pages beyond this introduction. It can be suggested, however, that Congreve set himself a double challenge – both to order intricate events so that what may seem to hinder the action only serves to accelerate it, and to fashion a graceful and stylised prose than can express the more sensational and impassioned moments of love intrigue.

Yet since drama was the dominant mode of the time, and Congreve was essentially a dramatic writer, it would be odd if this novel could not in some sense be construed as a play. It may not take place upon the London stage, but it is continually encircled with theatrical fire. There are monologues and desperate dialogues, strange meetings and stranger partings. Congreve himself declared that since 'all traditions must indisputably give place to the drama', he wished in *Incognita* 'to imitate dramatic writing, namely in the design, contexture and result of the plot'. As a result it is in part social comedy, in part sentimental tragedy, with a sprinkling of the elements of opera buffa to enliven a narrative which occasionally deviates into seriousness. It also anticipates some of the elements in Congreve's own drama, not least in the narrator's own ready and somewhat cynical wit, and foreshadows his invocation of 'Providence' in the most delicate and refined social situations. His is the theology of the drawing room – secrets will come out, and the wicked will eventually be unmasked.

Yet it can also withstand examination as prose fiction. It was, for a novel, something of a novelty. The narrator here takes on what was then a 'modern' role as an intrinsic aspect of the narrative; he is at once sardonic and sympathetic, a confidential friend who whispers a word in your ear. He remains in a certain sense detached from the action, so that the story itself can be viewed and admired as a work of pure artifice. It is in that sense a very skilful accomplishment indeed; it is both stylish and witty, with the observations of the narrator upon his own performance lending strength and coherence to a plot as fragile – if not as transparent – as gauze.

That is why certain critics have interpreted *Incognita* as a parody of conventional prose fiction, in which the promptings of romance are stronger than the claims of perceived reality. Congreve's scepticism has also been regarded as an element in that vogue for experiment and experimental science that pervaded the period. Such considerations must have a place in a proper reading of the narrative, but only a purblind critic would place them very high. We may quote Congreve's own words in the novel: 'I am always of the opinion with the learned,' he writes, 'if they speak first.' It is, in truth, a sophisticated social comedy of manners which prepares the way for the diverse talents of a Thackeray or a Sterne. Samuel Johnson once said of *Incognita*, rather mysteriously, that 'he would rather praise it than read it'. The readers of this volume now have the opportunity to do both.

– Peter Ackroyd, 2003

Incognita

To the honoured and worthily esteemed
Mrs Katharine Leveson[1]

Madam,
A clear wit, sound judgement and a merciful disposition are things so rarely united that it is almost inexcusable to entertain them with anything less excellent in its kind. My knowledge of you were a sufficient caution to me to avoid your censure of this trifle, had I not as entire a knowledge of your goodness. Since I have drawn my pen for a rencounter, I think it better to engage where, though there be skill enough to disarm me, there is too much generosity to wound; for so shall I have the saving reputation of an unsuccessful courage if I cannot make it a drawn battle. But methinks the comparison intimates something of a defiance, and savours of arrogance. Wherefore, since I am conscious to myself of a fear which I cannot put off, let me use the policy of cowards and lay this novel unarmed, naked and shivering at your feet so that if it should want merit to challenge protection, yet, as an object of charity, it may move compassion. It has been some diversion to me to write it; I wish it may prove such to you when you have an hour to throw away in reading of it. But this satisfaction I have at least beforehand: that in its greatest failings it may fly for pardon to that indulgence which you owe to the weakness of your friend – a title which I am proud you have thought me worthy of, and which I think can alone be superior to that
Your most humble and obliged servant

Cleophil[2]

THE PREFACE TO THE READER

Reader,

Some authors are so fond of a preface that they will write one though there be nothing more in it than an apology for itself. But to show thee that I am not one of those, I will make no apology for this, but do tell thee that I think it necessary to be prefixed to this trifle to prevent thy overlooking some little pains which I have taken in the composition of the following story.

Romances are generally composed of the constant loves and invincible courage of heroes, heroines, kings and queens, mortals of the first rank, and so forth, where lofty language, miraculous contingencies, and impossible performances elevate and surprise the reader into a giddy delight which leaves him flat upon the ground whenever he gives of, and vexes him to think how he has suffered himself to be pleased and transported, concerned and afflicted at the several passages which he has read, viz. these knights' success to their damsels' misfortunes, and suchlike, when he is forced to be very well convinced that 'tis all a lie.

Novels are of a more familiar nature: come near us, and represent to us intrigues in practice; delight us with accidents and odd events, but not such as are wholly unusual or unprecedented, such which not being so distant from our belief bring also the pleasure nearer us. Romances give more of wonder; novels more delight. And with reverence be it spoken, and the parallel kept at due distance, there is something of equality in the proportion which they bear in reference to one another with that between comedy and tragedy. But the drama is the long extracted from romance and history: 'tis the midwife to industry, and brings forth alive the conceptions of the brain. Minerva[3] *walks upon the stage before us, and we are more assured of the real presence of wit when it is delivered viva voce:*

Segnius irritant animos demissa per aurem,
Quam quae sunt oculis subiecta fidelibus, et quae
Ipse sibi tradit spectator.[4]

– Horace

Since all traditions must indisputably give place to the drama, and since there is no possibility of giving that life to the writing or repetition of a story which it has in the action, I resolved in another beauty to imitate dramatic writing, namely, in the design, contexture and result of the plot. I have not observed it before in a novel. Some I have seen begin with an unexpected accident, which has been the only surprising part of the story – cause enough to make the sequel look flat, tedious and insipid; for 'tis but reasonable the reader should expect it not to rise, at least to keep upon a level in the entertainment, for so he may be kept on in hopes that at some time or other it may mend, but the t'other is such a baulk to a man – 'tis carrying him upstairs to show him the dining room, and, after, forcing him to make a meal in the kitchen.

This I have not only endeavoured to avoid, but also have used a method for the contrary purpose. The design of the novel is obvious after the first meeting of Aurelian and Hippolito with Incognita and Leonora, and the difficulty is in bringing it to pass, maugre all apparent obstacles, within the compass of two days. How many probable casualties intervene in opposition to the main design, viz. of marrying two couples so oddly engaged in an intricate amour, I leave the reader at his leisure to consider, as also whether every obstacle does not, in the progress of the story, act as subservient to that purpose which at first it seems to oppose. In a comedy this would be called the unity of action; here it may pretend to no more than a unity of contrivance.[5]

The scene is continued in Florence from the commencement of the amour, and the time from first to last is but three days. If there be anything more in particular resembling the copy which I imitate (as the curious reader will soon perceive) I leave it to show itself, being very well satisfied how much more proper it had been for him to have found out this himself than for me to prepossess him with an opinion of something extraordinary in an essay begun and finished in the idler hours of a fortnight's time. For I can only esteem it a laborious idleness which is parent to so inconsiderable a birth.

I have gratified the bookseller in pretending an occasion for a preface. The other two persons concerned are the reader and myself, and if he be but pleased with what was produced for that end, my satisfaction follows of course, since it will be proportioned to his approbation or dislike.

Aurelian was the only son to a principal gentleman of Florence. The indulgence of his father prompted – and his wealth enabled him – to bestow a generous education upon him, whom he now began to look upon as the type of himself, an impression he had made in the gaiety and vigour of his youth before the rust of age had debilitated and obscured the splendour of the original. He was sensible that he ought not to be sparing in the adornment of him if he had resolution to beautify his own memory. Indeed, Don Fabio (for so was the old gentleman called) has been observed to have fixed his eyes upon Aurelian when much company has been at table, and have wept through earnestness of intention if nothing happened to divert the object. Whether it were for regret at the recollection of his former self, or for the joy he conceived in being, as it were, revived in the person of his son, I never took upon me to enquire, but supposed it might be sometimes one, and sometimes both together.

Aurelian, at the age of eighteen years, wanted nothing (but a beard) that the most accomplished cavalier in Florence could pretend to: he had been educated from twelve years old at Siena, where it seems his father kept a receiver, having a large income from the rents of several houses in that town. Don Fabio gave his servant orders that Aurelian should not be stinted in his expenses when he came up to years of discretion. By which means he was enabled, not only to keep company with, but also to confer many obligations upon strangers of quality and gentlemen who travelled from other countries into Italy, of which Siena never wanted store, being a town most delightfully situate upon a noble hill, and very well suiting with strangers at first by reason of the agreeableness and purity of the air. There also is the quaintness and delicacy of the Italian tongue most likely to be learned there, being many public professors of it in that place; and indeed the very vulgar of Siena do express themselves with an easiness and sweetness surprising, and even grateful, to their ears who understand not the language.

Here Aurelian contracted an acquaintance with persons of worth of several countries, but among the rest an intimacy with a gentleman of quality of Spain, and nephew to the Archbishop of Toledo, who had so wrought himself into the affections of Aurelian, through a conformity of temper, an equality in years, and something of resemblance in feature and proportion, that he looked upon him as his second self. Hippolito, on the other hand, was not ungrateful in return of friendship, but thought himself either alone or in ill company if Aurelian were absent. But his uncle having sent him to travel under the conduct of a governor, and the two years which limited his stay at Siena being expired, he was put in mind of his departure. His friend grew melancholy at the news, but considering that Hippolito had never seen Florence, he easily prevailed with him to make his first journey thither, whither he would accompany him, and perhaps prevail with his father to do the like throughout his travels.

They accordingly set out, but not being able easily to reach Florence the same night, they rested a league or two short at a villa of the Great Duke's called Poggio Imperiale[6] where they were informed by some of His Highness' servants that the nuptials of Donna Catharina (near kinswoman to the Great Duke) and Don Ferdinand de Roveri were to be solemnised the next day, and that extraordinary preparations had been making for some time past to illustrate the solemnity with balls and masques and other divertissements; that a tilting[7] had been proclaimed, and to that purpose scaffolds erected around the spacious court before the Church Di Santa Croce, where were usually seen all cavalcades and shows, performed by assemblies of the young nobility; that all mechanics and tradesmen were forbidden to work or expose any goods to sale for the space of three days, during which time all persons should be entertained at the Great Duke's cost, and public provision was to be made for the setting forth and furnishing a multitude of tables, with entertainment for all comers and goers, and several houses appointed for that use in all streets.

This account alarmed the spirits of our young travellers, and they were overjoyed at the prospect of pleasures they foresaw. Aurelian could not contain the satisfaction he conceived in the welcome Fortune had prepared for his dear Hippolito. In short, they both remembered so much of the pleasing relation had been made them that they forgot to sleep, and were up as soon as it was light, pounding at poor Signor Claudio's door (so was Hippolito's governor called) to rouse him, that no time might be lost till they were arrived at Florence, where they would furnish themselves with disguises and other accoutrements necessary for the prosecution of their design of sharing in the public merriment. The rather were they for going so early because Aurelian did not think fit to publish his being in town for a time, lest his father, knowing of it, might give some restraint to that loose they designed themselves.

Before sunrise they entered Florence at Porta Romana, attended only by two servants, the rest being left behind to avoid notice. But, alas! they needed not to have used half that caution for, early as it was, the streets were crowded with all sorts of people passing to and fro, and every man employed in something relating to the diversions to come, so that no notice was taken of anybody – a marquis and his train might have passed by as unregarded as a single fachin[8] or cobbler. Not a window in the streets but echoed the tuning of a lute or thrumming of a guitar; for, by the way, the inhabitants of Florence are strangely addicted to the love of music, insomuch that scarce their children can go before they can scratch some instrument or other. It was no unpleasing spectacle to our cavaliers (who, seeing they were not observed, resolved to make observations) to behold the diversity of figures and postures of many of these musicians. Here you should have an affected valet who mimicked the behaviour of his master, leaning carelessly against the window with his head on one side in a languishing posture, whining in a low mournful voice some dismal complaint while, from his sympathising theorbo, issued a base no less doleful to the hearers. In opposition to him was set up perhaps a cobbler, with the wretched skeleton of a guitar, battered and waxed together by his own industry, and who, with three strings out of tune and his own tearing hoarse voice, would rack attention from the neighbourhood to the great affliction of many more moderate practitioners, who, no doubt, were full as desirous to be heard.

By this time Aurelian's servant had taken a lodging and was returned to give his master an account of it. The cavaliers, grown weary of that ridiculous entertainment which was diverting at first sight, retired whither the lackey conducted them, who, according to their directions, had sought out one of the most obscure streets in the city. All that day, to the evening, was spent in sending from one broker's shop to another to furnish them with habits since they had not time to make any new.

There was, it happened, but one to be got rich enough to please our young gentlemen, so many were taken up upon this occasion. While they were in dispute and complimenting one another (Aurelian protesting that Hippolito should wear it, and he, on t'other hand, forswearing it as bitterly), a servant of Hippolito's came up and ended the controversy, telling them that he had met below with the *valet-de-chambre* of a gentleman who was one of the greatest gallants about the town, but was at this time in such a condition he could not possibly be at the entertainment. Whereupon the valet had designed to dress himself up in his master's apparel, and try his talent at Court; which he hearing, told him he would inform him how he might bestow the habit for some time much more to his profit if not to his pleasure, so acquainted him with the occasion his master had for it. Hippolito sent for the fellow up, who was not so fond of his design as not to be bought off it, but upon having his own demand granted for the use of it, brought it. It was very rich and, upon trial, as fit for Hippolito as if it had been made for him.

The ceremony was performed in the morning in the great dome, with all magnificence correspondent to the wealth of the Great Duke and the esteem he had for the noble pair. The next morning was to be a tilting, and the same night a masquing ball at Court. To omit the description of the universal joy (that had diffused itself through all the conduits of wine, which conveyed it in large measures to the people), and only relate those effects of it which concern our present adventurers: you must know that about the fall of the evening, and at that time when the equilibrium of day and night, for some time, holds the air in a gloomy suspense between an unwillingness to leave the light and a natural impulse into the dominion of darkness, about this time our heroes, shall I say, sallied or slunk out of their lodgings and steered towards the great palace whither, before they were arrived, such a prodigious number of torches were on fire that the day, by help of these auxiliary forces, seemed to continue its dominion. The owls and bats, apprehending their mistake in counting the hours, retired again to a convenient darkness; for Madam Night was no more to be seen than she was to be heard, and the chemists were of opinion that her fuliginous damps, rarefied by the abundance of flame, were evaporated.

Now the reader I suppose to be upon thorns at this and the like impertinent digressions, but let him alone and he'll come to himself, at which time I think fit to acquaint him that when I digress, I am at that time writing to please myself; when I continue the thread of the story, I write to please him. Supposing him a reasonable man, I conclude him satisfied to allow me this liberty, and so I proceed.

If our cavaliers were dazzled at the splendour they beheld without doors, what surprise, think you, must they be in when entering the palace they found even the lights there to be but so many foils to the bright eyes that flashed upon them at every turn.

A more glorious troop no occasion ever assembled; all the fair of Florence, with the most accomplished cavaliers, were present, and however Nature had been partial in bestowing on some better faces than others, Art was alike indulgent to all, and industriously supplied those defects she had left, giving some addition also to her greatest excellencies. Everybody appeared well shaped, as it is to be supposed; none who were conscious to themselves of any visible deformity would presume to come thither. Their apparel was equally glorious, though each differing in fancy. In short, our strangers were so well bred as to conclude from these apparent perfections that there was not a mask which did not at least hide the face of a cherubim.

Perhaps the ladies were not behindhand in return of a favourable opinion of them: for they were both well dressed, and had something inexpressibly pleasing in their air and mien, different from other people, and indeed differing from one another. They fancied that while they stood together they were more particularly taken notice of than any in the room, and being unwilling to be taken for strangers, which they thought they were, by reason of some whispering they observed near them, they agreed upon an hour of meeting after the company should be broken up, and so separately mingled with the thickest of the assembly.

Aurelian had fixed his eye upon a lady whom he had observed to have been a considerable time in close whisper with another woman. He expected with great impatience the result of that private conference that he might have an opportunity of engaging the lady whose person was so agreeable to him. At last he perceived they were broken off, and the other lady seemed to have taken her leave. He had taken no small pains in the meantime to put himself in a posture to accost the lady, which, no doubt, he had happily performed had he not been interrupted. But scarce had he acquitted himself of a preliminary bow (and which, I have heard him say, was the lowest that ever he made) and had just opened his lips to deliver himself of a small compliment, which, nevertheless, he was very big with, when he unluckily miscarried by the interposal of the same lady whose departure, not long before, he had so zealously prayed for. But, as Providence would have it, there was only some very small matter forgotten, which was recovered in a short whisper. The coast being again cleared, he took heart and bore up, and, striking sail, repeated his ceremony to the lady, who, having obligingly returned it, he accosted her in these or the like words:

'If I do not usurp a privilege reserved for someone more happy in your acquaintance, may I presume, madam, to entreat (for a while) the favour of your conversation, at least till the arrival of whom you expect, provided you are not tired of me before; for then upon the least intimation of uneasiness, I will not fail of doing myself the violence to withdraw for your release.'

The lady made him answer: she did not expect anybody, by which he might imagine her conversation not of value to be bespoke, and to afford it him were but further to convince him to her own cost. He replied she had already said enough to convince him of something he heartily wished might not be to his cost in the end. She pretended not to understand him, but told him if he already found himself grieved with her conversation, he would have sufficient reason to repent the rashness of his first demand before they had ended: for that now she intended to hold discourse with him on purpose to punish his unadvisedness in presuming upon a person whose dress and mien might not (maybe) be disagreeable to have wit.

'I must confess,' replied Aurelian, 'myself guilty of a presumption, and willingly submit to the punishment you intend; and though it be an aggravation of a crime to persevere in its justification, yet I cannot help defending an opinion in which now I am more confirmed, that probable conjectures may be made of the ingenious disposition of the mind, from the fancy and choice of apparel.'

'The humour I grant ye,' said the lady; 'or constitution of the person, whether melancholic or brisk. But I should hardly pass my censure upon so slight an indication of wit: for there is your brisk fool as well as your brisk man of sense, and so of the melancholic. I confess 'tis possible a fool may reveal himself by his dress in wearing something extravagantly singular and ridiculous, or in preposterous suiting of colours; but a decency of habit (which is all that men of best sense pretend to) may be acquired by custom and example, without putting the person to a superfluous expense of wit for the contrivance; and though there should be occasion for it, few are so unfortunate in their relations and acquaintance not to have some friend capable of giving them advice if they are not too ignorantly conceited to ask it.'

Aurelian was so pleased with the easiness and smartness of her expostulation that he forgot to make a reply when she seemed to expect it. But, being a woman of a quick apprehension and justly sensible of her own perfections, she soon perceived he did not grudge his attention. However she had a mind to put it upon him to turn the discourse, so went on upon the same subject.

'Signor,' said she, 'I have been looking round me, and by your maxim I cannot discover one fool in the company, for they are all well dressed.' This was spoken with an air of raillery that awakened the cavalier, who immediately made answer:

' 'Tis true, madam, we see there may be as much variety of good fancies as of faces, yet there may be many of both kinds borrowed and adulterate if enquired into. And as you were pleased to observe, the invention may be foreign to the person who puts it in practice; and as good an opinion as I have of an agreeable dress, I should be loath to answer for the wit of all about us.'

'I believe you,' says the lady, 'and hope you are convinced of your error, since you must allow it impossible to tell who of all this assembly did or did not make choice of their own apparel.'

'Not all,' said Aurelian. 'There is an ungainliness in some which betrays them. Look ye there,' says he, pointing to a lady who stood playing with the tassels of her girdle. 'I dare answer for that lady: though she be very well dressed, 'tis more than she knows.' His fair unknown could not forbear laughing at his particular distinction, and freely told him he had indeed lit upon one who knew as little as anybody in the room, herself excepted.

'Ah! madam,' replied Aurelian. 'You know everything in the world but your own perfections, and you only know not those because 'tis the top of perfection not to know them.'

'How?' replied the lady. 'I thought it had been the extremity of knowledge to know one's self.'

Aurelian had a little overstrained himself in that compliment, and I am of opinion would have been puzzled to have brought himself off readily. But, by good fortune, the music came into the room and gave him an opportunity to seem to decline an answer because the company prepared to dance. He only told her he was too mean a conquest for her wit who was already a slave to the charms of her person. She thanked him for his compliment, and briskly told him she ought to have made him a return in praise of his wit, but she hoped he was a man more happy than to be dissatisfied with any of his own endowments; and if it were so that he had not a just opinion of himself, she knew herself incapable of saying anything to beget one.

Aurelian did not know well what to make of this last reply, for he always abhorred anything that was conceited, with which this seemed to reproach him. But however modest he had been heretofore in his own thoughts, yet never was he so distrustful of his good behaviour as now, being rallied so by a person whom he took to be of judgement. Yet he resolved to take no notice, but with an air unconcerned and full of good humour entreated her to dance with him. She promised him to dance with nobody else, nor I believe had she inclination, for notwithstanding her tartness, she was upon equal terms with him as to the liking of each other's person and humour, and only gave those little hints to try his temper, there being certainly no greater sign of folly and ill breeding than to grow serious and concerned at anything spoken in raillery. For his part, he was strangely and insensibly fallen in love with her shape, wit and air, which, together with a white hand he had seen (perhaps not accidentally), were enough to have subdued a more stubborn heart than ever he was master of; and for her face, which he had not seen, he bestowed upon her the best his imagination could furnish him with.

I should by right now describe her dress, which was extremely agreeable and rich, but 'tis possible I might err in some material pin or other, in the sticking of which maybe the whole grace of the drapery depended.

Well, they danced several times together, and no less to the satisfaction of the whole company than of themselves, for at the end of each dance, some public note of applause or other was given to the graceful couple. Aurelian was amazed that among all that danced or stood in view he could not see Hippolito, but concluding that he had met with some pleasing conversation, and was withdrawn to some retired part of the room, he forbore his search till the mirth of that night should be over and the company ready to break up, where we will leave him for a while to see what became of his adventurous friend.

Hippolito, a little after he had parted with Aurelian, was got among a knot of ladies and cavaliers who were looking upon a large gold cup set with jewels in which His Royal

Highness had drunk to the prosperity of the new-married couple at dinner, and which afterwards he presented to his cousin, Donna Catharina. He among the rest was very intent, admiring the richness, workmanship and beauty of the cup, when a lady came behind him and, pulling him by the elbow, made a sign she would speak with him. Hippolito, who knew himself an utter stranger to Florence and everybody in it, immediately guessed she had mistaken him for her acquaintance, as indeed it happened. However, he resolved not to discover himself till he should be assured of it. Having followed her into a set window, remote from company, she addressed herself to him in this manner:

'Signor Don Lorenzo,' said she, 'I am overjoyed to see you are so speedily recovered of your wounds, which by report were much more dangerous than to have suffered your coming abroad so soon. But I must accuse you of great indiscretion in appearing in a habit which so many must needs remember you to have worn upon the like occasion not long ago – I mean at the marriage of Don Cynthio with your sister Atalanta. I do assure you, you were known by it, both to Juliana and myself, who was so far concerned for you as to desire me to tell you that her brother Don Fabritio, who saw you when you came in with another gentleman, had eyed you very narrowly, and is since gone out of the room, she knows not upon what design. However she would have you, for your own sake, be advised and circumspect when you depart this place lest you should be set upon unawares. You know the hatred Don Fabritio has borne you ever since you had the fortune to kill his kinsman in a duel.'

Here she paused as if expecting his reply, but Hippolito was so confounded that he stood mute, and, contemplating the hazard he had ignorantly brought himself into, forgot his design of informing the lady of her mistake. She, finding he made her no answer, went on.

'I perceive,' continued she, 'you are in some surprise at what I have related, and maybe, are doubtful of the truth, but I thought you had been better acquainted with your cousin Leonora's voice than to have forgotten it so soon. Yet, in complaisance to your ill memory, I will put you past doubt by showing you my face.'

With that she pulled off her mask, and discovered to Hippolito (now more amazed than ever) the most angelic face that he had ever beheld. He was just about to have made her some answer when, clapping on her mask again without giving him time, she, happily for him, pursued her discourse. (For 'tis odd but he had made some discovery of himself in the surprise he was in.)

Having taken him familiarly by the hand now she had made herself known to him, 'Cousin Lorenzo,' added she, 'you may perhaps have taken it unkindly that, during the time of your indisposition by reason of your wounds, I have not been to visit you. I do assure you it was not for want of any inclination I had, both to see and serve you to my power; but you are well acquainted with the severity of my father whom you know how lately you have disobliged. I am mighty glad that I have met with you here where I have had an opportunity to tell you what so much concerns your safety, which I am afraid you will not find in Florence, considering the great power Don Fabritio and his father, the Marquis of Viterbo, have in this city. I have another thing to inform you of: that whereas Don Fabio had interested himself in your cause, in opposition to the Marquis of Viterbo, by reason of the long animosity between them, all hopes of his countenance and assistance are defeated, for there has been a proposal of reconciliation made to both houses, and it is said it will be confirmed (as most such ancient quarrels are at last) by the marriage of Juliana, the Marquis' daughter, with Aurelian, son to Don Fabio: to which effect the old gentleman sent t'other day to Siena, where Aurelian has been educated, to hasten his coming to town. But the messenger returning this morning brought word that the same day he arrived at Siena, Aurelian had set out for Florence, in company with a young Spanish nobleman, his intimate friend. So it is believed they are both in town, and not unlikely in this room in masquerade.'

Hippolito could not forbear smiling to himself at these last words. For ever since the naming of Don Fabio he had been very attentive, but before, his thoughts were wholly taken up with the beauty of the face he had seen, and from the time she had taken him by the hand, a successive warmth and chillness had played about his heart, and surprised him with an unusual transport. He was in a hundred minds whether he should make her sensible of her error or no; but considering he could expect no further conference with her after he should discover himself, and that as yet he knew not of her place of abode, he resolved to humour the mistake a little further. Having her still by the hand, which he squeezed somewhat more eagerly than is usual for cousins to do, in a low and indistinguishable voice he let her know how much he held himself obliged to her, and, avoiding as many words as handsomely he could, at the same time entreated her to give him her advice towards the management of himself in this affair.

Leonora, who never from the beginning had entertained the least scruple of distrust, imagined he spoke faintly as not being yet perfectly recovered in his strength; and withal considering that the heat of the room, by reason of the crowd, might be uneasy to a person in his condition, she kindly told him that if he were as inclinable to dispense with the remainder of that night's diversion as she was, and had no other engagement upon him, by her consent they should both steal out of the assembly and go to her house, where they might with more freedom discourse about a business of that importance, and where he might take something to refresh himself if he were (as she conceived him to be) indisposed with his long standing.

Judge you whether the proposal were acceptable to Hippolito or no! He had been ruminating with himself how to bring something like this about, and had almost despaired of it, when of a sudden he found the success of his design had prevented his own endeavours. He told his cousin in the same key as before that he was unwilling to be the occasion of her divorce from so much good company, but for his own part he was afraid he had presumed too much upon his recovery in coming abroad so soon, and that he found himself so unwell, he feared he should be quickly forced to retire. Leonora stayed not to make him any other reply, only tipped him upon the arm, and bid him follow her at a convenient distance to avoid observation.

Whoever had seen the joy that was in Hippolito's countenance and the sprightliness with which he followed his beautiful conductress would scarce have taken him for a person grieved with uncured wounds. She led him down a back pair of stairs into one of the palace gardens which had a door opening into the piazza, not far from where Don Mario, her father, lived. They had little discourse by the way, which gave Hippolito time to consider of the best way of discovering himself. A thousand things came into his head in a minute, yet nothing that pleased him: and after so many contrivances as he had formed for the discovery of himself, he found it more rational for him not to reveal himself at all that night, since he could not foresee what effect the surprise would have, she must needs be in, at the appearance of a stranger whom she had never seen before, yet whom she had treated so familiarly. He knew women were apt to shriek or swoon upon such occasions, and should she happen to do either, he might be at a loss how to bring himself off. He thought he might easily pretend to be indisposed somewhat more than ordinary, and so make an excuse to go to his own lodging. It came into his head, too, that under pretence of giving her an account of his health, he might enquire of her the means how a letter might be conveyed to her the next morning, wherein he might inform her gently of her mistake, and insinuate something of that passion he had conceived, which he was sure he could not have opportunity to speak of if he bluntly revealed himself.

He had just resolved upon this method as they were come to the great gates of the court when Leonora, stopping to let him go in before her, he of a sudden fetched his breath violently as if some stitch or twingeing smart had just then assaulted him. She enquired the matter of him, and advised him to make haste into the house that he might sit down and rest him. He told her he found himself so ill that he judged it more convenient for him to go home while he was in a condition to move, for he feared if he should once settle himself to rest he might not be able to stir. She was much troubled and would have had a chair made ready and servants to carry him home, but he made answer he would not have any of her father's servants know of his being abroad, and that just now he had an interval of ease which he hoped would continue till he made a shift to reach his own lodgings. Yet if she pleased to inform him how he might give an account of himself the next morning, in a line or two, he would not fail to give her the thanks due to her great kindness; and withal, would let her know something which would not a little surprise her, though now he had not time to acquaint her with it.

She showed him a little window at the corner of the house where one should wait to receive his letter, and was just taking her leave of him when, seeing him search hastily in his pocket, she asked him if he missed anything. He told her he thought a wound which was not thoroughly healed bled a little, and that he had lost his handkerchief. His design took; for she immediately gave him hers, which indeed accordingly he applied to the only wound he was then grieved with, which though it went quite through his heart, yet, thank God, was not mortal. He was not a little rejoiced at his good fortune in getting so early a favour from his mistress, and notwithstanding the violence he did himself to personate a sick man, he could not forbear giving some symptoms of an extraordinary content, and telling her that he did not doubt to receive a considerable proportion of ease from the application of what had so often kissed her fair hand. Leonora, who did not suspect the compliment, told him she should be heartily glad if that or anything in her power might contribute to his recovery; and wishing him well home, went into her house, as much troubled for her cousin as he was joyful for his mistress.

Hippolito, as soon as she was gone in, began to make his remarks about the house, walking round the great court, viewing the gardens and all the passages leading to that side of the piazza. Having sufficiently informed himself, with a heart full of love, and a head full of stratagem, he walked towards his lodging, impatient till the arrival of Aurelian that he might give himself vent.

In which interim, let me take the liberty to digress a little, and tell the reader something which I do not doubt he has apprehended himself long ago, if he be not the dullest reader in the world. Yet only for order's sake, let me tell him, I say, that a young gentleman (cousin to the aforesaid Don Fabritio) happened one night to have some words at a gaming-house with one Lorenzo which created a quarrel of fatal consequence to the former – who was killed upon the spot – and likely to be so to the latter, who was very desperately wounded. Fabritio, being much concerned for his kinsman, vowed revenge (according to the ancient and laudable custom of Italy) upon Lorenzo if he survived, or in case of his death (if it should happen to anticipate that much more swingeing death which he had in store for him) upon his next of kin, and so to descend lineally like an English estate to all the heirs male of this family. This same Fabritio had indeed (as Leonora told Hippolito) taken particular notice of him from his first entrance into the room, and was so far doubtful as to go out immediately himself and make enquiry concerning Lorenzo, but was quickly informed of the greatness of his error in believing a man to be abroad who was so ill of his wounds that they now despaired of his recovery; and thereupon returned to the ball very well satisfied, but not before Leonora and Hippolito were departed.

So, Reader, having now discharged my conscience of a small discovery which I thought myself obliged to make to thee, I proceed to tell thee that our friend Aurelian had by this time danced himself into a net which he neither could nor, which is worse, desired to untangle. His soul was charmed to the movement of her body: an air so graceful, so sweet, so easy and so great, he had never seen. She had something of majesty in her which appeared to be born with her, and though it struck an awe into the beholders, yet was it sweetened with a familiarity of behaviour which rendered it agreeable to everybody. The grandeur of her mien was not stiff, but unstudied and unforced, mixed with a simplicity; free, yet not loose nor affected. If the former seemed to condescend, the latter seemed to aspire; and both to unite in the centre of perfection. Every turn she gave in dancing snatched Aurelian into a rapture, and he had like to have been out two or three times with the following his eyes, which she led about as slaves to her heels. As soon as they had done dancing, he began to complain of his want of breath and lungs to speak sufficiently in her commendation. She smilingly told him he did ill to dance so much then; yet in consideration of the pains he had taken more than ordinary upon her account she would bate him a great deal of compliment – but with this proviso: that he was to discover to her who he was.

Aurelian was unwilling for the present to own himself to be really the man he was when a sudden thought came into his head to take upon him the name and character of Hippolito who he was sure was not known in Florence. He thereupon, after a little pause, pretended to recall himself in this manner:

'Madam, it is no small demonstration of the entire resignation which I have made of my heart to your chains, since the secrets of it are no longer in my power. I confess I only took Florence in my way, not designing any longer residence than should be requisite to inform the curiosity of a traveller of the rarities of the place. Whether happiness or misery will be the consequence of that curiosity, I am yet in fear and submit to your determination. But sure I am not to depart Florence till you have made me the most miserable man in it and refuse me the fatal kindness of dying at your feet. I am by birth a Spaniard, of the City of Toledo; my name Hippolito di Saviolina. I was yesterday a man free as Nature made the first; today I am fallen into a captivity which must continue with my life, and which it is in your power to make much dearer to me. Thus in obedience to your commands, and contrary to my resolution of remaining unknown in this place, I have informed you, madam, what I am. What I shall be, I desire to know from you. At least, I hope, the free discovery I have made of myself will encourage you to trust me with the knowledge of your person.' Here a low bow and a deep sigh put an end to his discourse, and signified his expectation of her reply, which was to this purpose – (But I had forgot to tell you that Aurelian kept off his mask from the time that he told her he was of Spain, till the period of his relation.)

'Had I thought,' said she, 'that my curiosity would have brought me in debt, I should certainly have forborne it; or at least have agreed with you beforehand about the rate of your discovery. Then I had not brought myself to the inconvenience of being censured, either of too much easiness or reservedness. But to avoid, as much as I can, the extremity of either, I am resolved but to discover myself in part, and will endeavour to give you as little occasion as I can either to boast of, or ridicule the behaviour of the women of Florence in your travels.'

Aurelian interrupted her, and swore very solemnly (and the more heartily, I believe, because he then indeed spoke truth) that he would make Florence the place of his abode, whatever concerns he had elsewhere. She advised him to be cautious how he swore to his expressions of gallantry, and further told him she now hoped she should make him a return to all the fine things he had said, since she gave him his choice whether he would know who she was or see her face. Aurelian, who was really in love, and in whom consideration would have been a crime, greedily embraced the latter since she assured him at that time he should not know both.

Well, what followed? Why, she pulled off her mask, and appeared to him at once in the glory of beauty. But who can tell the astonishment Aurelian felt? He was for a time senseless; admiration had suppressed his speech, and his eyes were entangled in light. In short, to be made sensible of his condition we must conceive some idea of what he beheld, which is not to be imagined till seen, nor then to be expressed. (Now see the impertinence and conceitedness of an author who will have a fling at a description which he has prefaced with an impossibility.) One might have seen something in her composition resembling the formation of Epicurus his world, as if every atom of beauty had concurred to unite an excellency.[9] Had that curious painter lived in her days, he might have avoided his painful search when he collected from the choicest pieces the most choice features, and by a due disposition and judicious symmetry of those exquisite parts, made one whole and perfect Venus. Nature seemed here to have played the plagiarist and to have moulded into substance the most refined thoughts of inspired poets. Her eyes diffused rays comfortable as warmth, and piercing as the light; they would have worked a passage through the straightest pores and, with a delicious heat, have played about the most obdurate frozen heart until 'twere melted down to love. Such majesty and affability were in her looks; so alluring, yet commanding was her presence that it mingled awe with love, kindling a flame which trembled to aspire. She had danced much, which, together with her being close masked, gave her a tincture of carnation more than ordinary. But Aurelian (from whom I had every tittle of her description) fancied he saw a little nest of Cupids break from the tresses of her hair, and every one officiously betake himself to his task. Some fanned with their downy wings her glowing cheeks, while others brushed the balmy dew from off her face leaving alone a heavenly moisture blubbing on her lips, on which they drank and revelled for their pains. Nay, so particular were their allotments in her service that Aurelian was very positive a young Cupid, who was but just pen-feathered, employed his naked quills to pick her teeth. And a thousand other things his transport represented to him which none but lovers who have experience of such visions will believe.

As soon as he awakened and found his speech come to him, he employed it to this effect:

'’Tis enough that I have seen a divinity – nothing but mercy can inhabit these perfections – their utmost rigour brings a death preferable to any life but what they give. Use me, madam, as you please; for by your fair self, I cannot think a bliss beyond what now I feel. – You wound with pleasure, and if you kill it must be with transport. – Ah! Yet methinks to live. – O Heaven! to have life pronounced by those blessed lips – did they not inspire where they command, it were an immediate death of joy.'

Aurelian was growing a little too loud with his admiration, had she not just then interrupted him by clapping on her mask and telling him they should be observed if he proceeded in his extravagance; and, withal, that his passion was too sudden to be real, and too violent to be lasting. He replied, indeed, it might not be very lasting (with a submissive mournful voice), but it would continue during his life. That it was sudden, he denied, for she had raised it by degrees from his first sight of her, by a continued discovery of charms, in her mien and conversation till she thought fit to set fire to the train she had laid by the lightning of her face; and then he could not help it if he were blown up.

He begged her to believe the sincerity of his passion, at least to enjoin him something which might tend to the convincing of her incredulity. She said she should find a time to make some trials of him; but for the first she charged him not to follow or observe her after the dissolution of the assembly. He promised to obey, and entreated her to tell him but her name that he might have recourse to that in his affliction for her absence, if he were able to survive it. She desired him to live by all means, and if he must have a name to play with, to call her Incognita till he were better informed.

The company breaking up, she took her leave, and at his earnest entreaty gave him a short vision of her face which, then dressed in an obliging smile, caused another fit of transport which lasted till she was gone out of sight.

Aurelian gathered up his spirits, and walked slowly towards his lodging, never remembering that he had lost Hippolito till, upon turning the corner of a street, he heard a noise of fighting, and, coming near, saw a man make a vigorous defence against two who pressed violently upon him. He then thought of Hippolito, and fancying he saw the glimmering of diamond buttons such as Hippolito had upon the sleeves of his habit, immediately drew to his assistance, and with that eagerness and resolution that the assailants, finding their unmanly odds defeated, took to their heels. The person rescued by the generous help of Aurelian came towards him. But, as he would have stooped to have saluted him, dropped, fainting at his feet. Aurelian, now he was so near him, perceived plainly Hippolito's habit, and stepped hastily to take him up.

Just as some of the guards (who were going the rounds, apprehensive of such disorders in a universal merriment) came up to him with lights, and had taken prisoner the two men whom they met with their swords drawn, when looking in the face of the wounded man, he found it was not Hippolito, but his governor Claudio, in the habit he had worn at the ball. He was extremely surprised, as were the prisoners, who confessed their design to have been upon Lorenzo, grounding their mistake upon the habit which was known to have been his. They were two men who formerly had been servants to him whom Lorenzo had unfortunately slain.

They made a shift to bring Claudio to himself, and, part of the guard carrying off the prisoners whom Aurelian desired they would secure, the rest accompanied him bearing Claudio in their arms to his lodging. He had not patience to forbear asking for Hippolito by the way, whom Claudio assured him he had left safe in his chamber above two hours since; that his coming home so long before the divertissements were ended, and undressing himself, had given him the unhappy curiosity to put on his habit and go to the palace, in his return from whence he was set upon in the manner he found him, which if he recovered, he must own his life indebted to his timely assistance.

Being come to the house, they carried him to his bed, and having sent for surgeons, Aurelian rewarded and dismissed the guard. He stayed the dressing of Claudio's wounds, which were many, though they hoped none mortal, and leaving him to his rest, went to give Hippolito an account of what had happened, whom he found with a table before him, leaning upon both his elbows, his face covered with his hands, and so motionless that Aurelian concluded he was asleep.

Seeing several papers lie before him, half written and blotted out again, he thought to steal softly to the table and discover what he had been employed about. Just as he reached forth his hand to take up one of the papers, Hippolito started up so on the sudden as surprised Aurelian and made him leap back. Hippolito, on the other hand, not supposing that anybody had been near him, was so disordered with the appearance of a man at his elbow (whom his amazement did not permit him to distinguish), that he leapt hastily to his sword, and in turning him about, overthrew the stand and candles. Here were they both left in the dark, Hippolito groping about with his sword, and thrusting at every chair that he felt oppose him. Aurelian was scarce come to himself when, thinking to step back towards the door that he might inform his friend of his mistake without exposing himself to his blind fury, Hippolito heard him stir and made a full thrust with such violence that the hilt of the sword meeting with Aurelian's breast beat him down, and Hippolito atop of him, as a servant, alarmed with the noise, came into the chamber with a light.

The fellow trembled and thought they were both dead, till Hippolito, raising himself to see whom he had got under him, swooned away upon the discovery of his friend. But such was the extraordinary care of Providence in directing the sword that it only passed under his arm, giving no wound to Aurelian but a little bruise between his shoulder and breast with the hilt. He got up, scarce recovered of his fright, and by the help of the servant, laid Hippolito upon the bed, who, when he was come to himself, could hardly be persuaded that his friend was before him and alive till he showed him his breast, where was nothing of a wound. Hippolito begged his pardon a thousand times, and cursed himself as often, who was so near to committing the last execrable act of amicide.

They dismissed the fellow, and, with many embraces, congratulated their fortunate delivery from the mischief which came so near them, each blaming himself as the occasion: Aurelian accusing his own unadvisedness in stealing upon Hippolito; Hippolito blaming his own temerity and weakness in being so easily frighted to disorder and, last of all, his blindness in not knowing his dearest friend. But there he gave a sigh, and, passionately taking Aurelian by the hand, cried, 'Ah! my friend, love is indeed blind when it would not suffer me to see you.' There arose another sigh. A sympathy seized Aurelian immediately (for, by the way, sighing is as catching among lovers as yawning among the vulgar). Beside, hearing the name of love made him fetch such a sigh that Hippolito's were but fly-blows in comparison – that was answered with all the might Hippolito had – Aurelian plied him close till they were both out of breath. Thus not a word passed, though each wondered why the other sighed, at last concluded it to be only complaisance to one another.

Aurelian broke the silence by telling him the misfortune of his governor. Hippolito rejoiced as at the luckiest accident which could have befallen him. Aurelian wondered at his unseasonable mirth, and demanded the cause of it. He answered it would necessitate his longer stay in Florence, and for ought he knew, be the means of bringing a happy period to his amour. His friend thought him to be little better than a madman when he perceived him of a sudden snatch out of his bosom a handkerchief, which having kissed with a great deal of ardour, he took Aurelian by the hand, and smiling at the surprise he saw him in:

'Your Florentine Cupid is certainly,' said he, 'the most expert in the world. I have, since I saw you, beheld the most beautiful of women. I am fallen desperately in love with her, and those papers which you see so blotted and scattered are but so many essays which I have made to the declaration of my passion. And this handkerchief which I so zealously caress is the inestimable token which I have to make myself known to her. O Leonora!' continued he, 'how hast thou stamped thine image on my soul! How much dearer am I to myself since I have had thy heavenly form in keeping! Now, my Aurelian, I am worthy thee: my exalted love has dignified me and raised me far above thy poor former despicable Hippolito.'

Aurelian, seeing the rapture he was in, thought it in vain to expect a settled relation of the adventure, so was reaching to the table for some of the papers, but Hippolito told him if he would have a little patience he would acquaint him with the whole matter, and thereupon told him word for word how he was mistaken for Lorenzo, and his management of himself. Aurelian commended his prudence in not discovering himself, and told him, if he could spare so much time from the contemplation of his mistress, he would inform him of an adventure, though not so accidental, yet of as great concern to his own future happiness. So related all that had happened to him with his beautiful Incognita.

Having ended the story, they began to consider of the means they were to use towards a review of their mistresses. Aurelian was confounded at the difficulty he conceived on his part. He understood from Hippolito's adventure that his father knew of his being in town, whom he must unavoidably disoblige if he yet concealed himself, and disobey if he came into his sight; for he had already entertained an aversion for Juliana in apprehension of her being imposed on him. His Incognita was rooted in his heart, yet could he not comfort himself with any hopes when he should see her: he knew not where she lived, and she had made him no promise of a second conference. Then did he repent his inconsiderate choice in preferring the momentary vision of her face to a certain intelligence of her person. Every thought that succeeded distracted him, and all the hopes he could presume upon were within compass of the two days' merriment yet to come, for which space he hoped he might excuse his remaining concealed to his father.

Hippolito, on the other side (though Aurelian thought him in a much better way), was no less afflicted for himself. The difficulties which he saw in his friend's circumstances put him upon finding out a great many more in his own than really there were. But what terrified him most of all was his being an utter stranger to Leonora; she had not the least knowledge of him but through mistake, and consequently could form no idea of him to his advantage. He looked upon it as an unlucky thought in Aurelian to take upon him his name, since possibly the two ladies were acquainted, and should they communicate to each other their adventures, they might both reasonably suffer in their opinions and be thought guilty of falsehood since it would appear to them as one person pretending to two. Aurelian told him there was but one remedy for that, which was for Hippolito, in the same manner that he had done, to make use of his name when he wrote to Leonora, and use what arguments he could to persuade her to secrecy, lest his father should know of the reason which kept him concealed in town. And it was likely, though perhaps she might not immediately entertain his passion, yet she would out of generosity conceal what was hidden only for her sake.

Well, this was concluded on after a great many other reasons used on either side in favour of the contrivance: they at last argued themselves into a belief that Fortune had befriended them with a better plot than their regular thinking could have contrived. So, soon had they convinced themselves in what they were willing to believe.

Aurelian laid himself down to rest, that is, upon the bed, for he was a better lover than to pretend to sleep that night, while Hippolito set himself again to frame his letter designed for Leonora. He wrote several, at last pitched upon one, and very probably the worst, as you may guess when you read it in its proper place. It was break of day when the servant, who had been employed all the foregoing day in procuring accoutrements for the two cavaliers to appear in at the tilting, came into the room, and told them all the young gentlemen in the town were trying their equipage and preparing to be early in the lists. They made themselves ready with all expedition at the alarm, and Hippolito, having made a visit to his governor, dispatched a messenger with the letter and directions to

Leonora. At the signal agreed upon, the casement was opened and a string let down, to which the bearer, having fastened the letter, saw it drawn up and returned.

It were a vain attempt to describe Leonora's surprise when she read the superscription: *The unfortunate Aurelian, to the beautiful Leonora*. After she was a little recovered from her amazement, she recollected to herself all the passages between her and her supposed cousin, and immediately concluded him to be Aurelian. Then several little circumstances, which she thought might have been sufficient to have convinced her, represented themselves to her; and she was in a strange uneasiness to think of her free carriage to a stranger. She was once in a mind to have burnt the letter, or to have stayed for an opportunity to send it again. But she was a woman, and her curiosity opposed itself to all thoughts of that nature. At length, with a firm resolution, she opened it, and found word for word, what is underwritten.

The Letter

Madam,
If your fair eyes upon the breaking up of this meet with somewhat too quick a surprise, make thence, I beseech you, some reflection upon the condition I must needs have been in at the sudden appearance of that sun of beauty which at once shone so full upon my soul. I could not immediately disengage myself from that maze of charms to let you know how unworthy a captive your eyes had made through mistake. Sure, madam, you cannot but remember my

disorder, of which your innocent (innocent, though perhaps – to me – fatal) error made a charitable (but wide) construction. Your tongue pursued the victory of your eyes, and you did not give me time to rally my poor disordered senses so as to make a tolerable retreat. Pardon, madam, the continuation of the deceit, and call it not so that I appeared to be other than myself: for Heaven knows I was not then myself, nor am I now my own. You told me something that concerned me nearly, as to a marriage my father designed me, and much more nearly in being told by you. For Heaven's sake, disclose not to anybody your knowledge of me that I may not be forced to an immediate act of disobedience. For if my future services and inviolate love cannot recommend me to your favour, I shall find more comfort in the cold embraces of a grave than in the arms of the never-so-much admired (but by me dreaded) Juliana. Think, madam, of those severe circumstances I lie under; and withal I beg you, think it is in your power, and only in your power, to make them happy as my wishes, or much more miserable than I am able to imagine. That dear, inestimable (though undesigned) favour which I received from you shall this day distinguish me from the crowd of your admirers; that which I really applied to my inward bleeding wound, the welcome wound which you have made, and which, unless from you, does wish no cure; then pardon and have pity on, O adored Leonora, him, who is yours by creation as he is Heaven's, though never so unworthy. Have pity on

Your

Aurelian

She read the letter over and over, then flung it by, then read it again. The novelty of the adventure made her repeat her curiosity and take more than ordinary pains to understand it. At last her familiarity with the expressions grew to an intimacy, and what she at first permitted she now began to like. She thought there was something in it a little more serious than to be barely gallantry. She wondered at her own blindness, and fancied she could remember something of a more becoming air in the stranger than was usual to Lorenzo. This thought was parent to another of the same kind, till a long chain successively had birth, and every one somewhat more than the others, in favour of the supposed Aurelian. She reflected upon his discretion in deferring the discovery of himself till a little time had, as it were, weaned her from her persuasion, and by removing her further from her mistake, had prepared her for a full and determinate convincement. She thought his behaviour, in personating a sick man so readily, upon the first hint was not amiss, and smiled to think of his excuse to procure her handkerchief; and last of all, his sifting out the means to write to her, which he had done with that modesty and respect, she could not tell how to find fault with it.

She had proceeded thus far in a maze of thought when she started to find herself so lost to her reason, and would have trod back again that path of deluding fancy, accusing herself of fondness and inconsiderate easiness in giving credit to the letter of a person whose face she never saw, and whose first acquaintance with her was a treachery, and he who could so readily deliver his tongue of a lie upon a surprise, was scarce to be trusted when he had sufficient time allowed him to beget a fiction and means to perfect the birth.

How did she know this to be Aurelian, if he were? Nay further, put it to the extremity, what if she should upon further conversation with him proceed to love him? What hopes were there for her? Or how could she consent to marry a man already destined for another woman? Nay, a woman that was her friend, whose marrying with him was to complete the happy reconciliation of two noble families, and which might prevent the effusion of much blood likely to be shed in that quarrel. Besides, she should incur share of the guilt which he would draw upon him by disobedience to his father, whom she was sure would not be consenting to it.

'Tis strange now, but all accounts agree that just here Leonora, who had run like a violent stream against Aurelian hitherto, now retorted with as much precipitation in his favour. I could never get anybody to give me a satisfactory reason for her sudden and dexterous change of opinion just at that stop, which made me conclude she could not help it, and that Nature boiled over in her at that time when it had so fair an opportunity to show itself. For Leonora it seems was a woman beautiful, and otherwise of an excellent disposition, but in the bottom a very woman. This last objection, this opportunity of persuading man to disobedience, determined the matter in favour of Aurelian more than all his excellencies and qualifications, take him as Aurelian or Hippolito or both together.

Well, the spirit of contradiction and of Eve was strong in her, and she was in a fair way to love Aurelian for she liked him already. That it was Aurelian she no longer doubted, for had it been a villain who had only taken his name upon him for any ill designs, he would never have slipped so favourable an opportunity as when they were alone and in the night coming through the garden and broad space before the piazza. In short, thus much she resolved, at least to conceal the knowledge she had of him as he had entreated her in his letter, and to make particular remarks of his behaviour that day in the lists, which should it happen to charm her with an absolute liking of his person, she resolved to dress herself to the best advantage, and mustering up all her graces, out of pure revenge, to kill him downright.

I would not have the reader now be impertinent and look upon this to be force, or a whim of the author's that a woman should proceed so far in her approbation of a man whom she never saw, that it is impossible, therefore ridiculous, to suppose it. Let me tell such a critic that he knows nothing of the sex if he does not know that woman may be taken with the character and description of a man, when general and extraordinary, that she may be prepossessed with an agreeable idea of his person and conversation; and though she cannot imagine his real features or manner of wit, yet she has a general notion of what is called a fine gentleman, and is prepared to like such a one who does not disagree with that character. Aurelian, as he bore a very fair character, so was he extremely deserving to make it good, which otherwise might have been to his prejudice; for oftentimes, through an imprudent indulgence to our friend's merit, we give so large a description of his excellencies that people make more room in their expectation than the intrinsic worth of the man will fill, which renders him so much the more despicable as there is emptiness to spare. 'Tis certain, though, the women seldom find that out; for though they do not see so much in a man as was promised, yet they will be so kind to imagine he has some hidden excellencies, which time may discover to them, so are content to allow him a considerable share of their esteem, and take him into favour upon tick[10]. Aurelian, as he had good credit, so he had a good stock to support it, and his person was a good promising security for the payment of any obligation he could lie under to the fair sex. Hippolito, who at this time was our Aurelian, did not at all lessen him in appearing for him, so that although Leonora was indeed mistaken, she could not be said to be much in the wrong. I could find in my heart to beg the reader's pardon for this digression if I thought he would be sensible of the civility; for I promise him I do not intend to do it again throughout the story, though I make never so many, and though he take them never so ill. But because I began this upon a bare supposition of his impertinence, which might be somewhat impertinent in me to suppose, I do, and hope to, make him amends by telling him that by the time Leonora was dressed, several ladies of her acquaintance came to accompany her to the place designed for the tilting, where we will leave them drinking chocolate till 'tis time for them to go.

Our cavaliers had by good fortune provided themselves of two curious suits of light armour, finely enamelled and gilt. Hippolito had sent to Poggio Imperiale for a couple of fine bred horses which he had left there with the rest of his train at his entrance into Florence. Mounted on these and every way well equipped, they took their way, attended only by two lackeys, towards the Church di Santa Croce, before which they were to perform their exercises of chivalry. Hippolito wore upon his helm a large plume of crimson feathers, in the midst of which was artificially placed Leonora's handkerchief. His armour was gilt, and enamelled with green and crimson. Aurelian was not so happy as to wear any token to recommend him to the notice of his mistress, so had only a plume of sky colour and white feathers, suitable to his armour, which was silver enamelled with azure. I shall not describe the habits of any other cavaliers, or of the ladies; let it suffice to tell the reader they were all very fine and very glorious, and let him dress them in what is most agreeable to his own fancy.

Our gallants entered the lists, and having made their obeisance to His Highness, turned round to salute and view the company. The scaffold was circular so that there was no end of the delightful prospect. It seemed a glory of beauty which shone around the admiring beholders. Our lovers soon perceived the stars which were to rule their destiny, which sparkled a lustre beyond all the inferior constellations, and seemed like two suns to distribute light to all the planets in that heavenly sphere. Leonora knew her slave by his badge, and blushed till the lilies and roses in her cheeks had resemblance to the plume of crimson and white handkerchief in Hippolito's crest. He made her a low bow, and reined his horse back with an extraordinary grace into a respectful retreat. Aurelian saw his angel, his beautiful Incognita, and had no other way to make himself known to her but by saluting and bowing to her after the Spanish mode. She guessed him by it to be her new servant Hippolito, and signified her apprehension by making him a more particular and obliging return than to any of the cavaliers who had saluted her before.

The exercise that was to be performed was in general a running at the ring, and afterwards two cavaliers undertook to defend the beauty of Donna Catharina against all who would not allow her pre-eminence of their mistresses. This thing was only designed for show and form, none presuming that anybody would put so great an affront upon the bride and Duke's kinswoman as to dispute her pretensions to the first place in the Court of Venus. But here our cavaliers were under a mistake. For seeing a large shield carried before two knights with a lady painted upon it, not knowing who, but reading the inscription which was (in large gold letters) '*Above the Insolence of Competition*', they thought themselves obliged, especially in the presence of their mistresses, to vindicate their beauty, and were just spurring on to engage the champions when a gentleman, stopping them, told them their mistake: that it was the picture of Donna Catharina, and a particular honour done to her by His Highness' commands, and not to be disputed.

Upon this they would have returned to their post, much concerned for their mistake, but notice being taken by Don Ferdinand of some show of opposition that was made, he would have begged leave of the Duke to have maintained his lady's honour against the insolence of those cavaliers; but the Duke would by no means permit it. They were arguing about it when one of them came up, before whom the shield was borne, and demanded His

Highness' permission to inform those gentlemen better of their mistake by giving them the foil. By the intercession of Don Ferdinand, leave was given them, whereupon a civil challenge was sent to the two strangers, informing them of their error, and withal telling them they must either maintain it by force of arms, or make a public acknowledgement by riding bareheaded before the picture once round the lists.

The stranger-cavaliers remonstrated to the Duke how sensible they were of their error, and though they would not justify it, yet they could not decline the combat, being pressed to it beyond an honourable refusal. To the bride they sent a compliment, wherein, having first begged her pardon for not knowing her picture, they gave her to understand that now they were not about to dispute her undoubted right to the crown of beauty, but the honour of being her champions was the prize they fought for, which they thought themselves as able to maintain as any other pretenders. Wherefore they prayed her that if Fortune so far befriended their endeavours as to make them victors, that they might receive no other reward but to be crowned with the titles of their adversaries, and be ever after esteemed as her most humble servants. The excuse was so handsomely designed, and much better expressed than it is here, that it took effect. The Duke, Don Ferdinand and his lady were so well satisfied with it as to grant their request.

While the running at the ring lasted, our cavaliers alternately bore away great share of the honour. That sport ended, marshals were appointed for the field, and everything in great form settled for the combat. The cavaliers were all in good earnest, but orders were given to bring them blunted lances, and to forbid the drawing of a sword upon pain of His Highness' displeasure.

The trumpets sounded and they began their course: the ladies' hearts, particularly the Incognita and Leonora's, beat time to the horses' hoofs, and hope and fear made a mock fight within their tender breasts, each wishing and doubting success where she liked. But as the generality of their prayers were for the graceful strangers, they accordingly succeeded. Aurelian's adversary was unhorsed in the first encounter, and Hippolito's lost both stirrups and dropped his lance to save himself. The honour of the field was immediately granted to them, and Donna Catharina sent them both favours, which she prayed them to wear as her knights.

The crowd breaking up, our cavaliers made a shift to steal off unmarked, save by the watchful Leonora and Incognita, whose eyes were never off from their respective servants. There was enquiry made for them, but to no purpose; for they – to prevent their being discovered – had prepared another house, distant from their lodging, where a servant attended to disarm them, and another carried back their horses to the villa while they walked unsuspected to their lodging. But Incognita had given command to a page to dog them till the evening, at a distance, and bring her word where they were latest housed. While several conjectures passed among the company – who were all gone to dinner at the palace – who those cavaliers should be, Don Fabio thought himself the only man able to guess; for he knew for certain that his son and Hippolito were both in town, and was well enough pleased with his humour of remaining incognito till the diversions should be over, believing then that the surprise of his discovery would add much to the gallantry he had shown in masquerade. But, hearing the extraordinary liking that everybody expressed, and in a particular manner, the Great Duke himself, to the persons and behaviour of the unknown cavaliers, the old gentleman could not forbear the vanity to tell His Highness that he believed he had an interest in one of the gentlemen, whom he was pleased to honour with so favourable a character; and told him what reason he had to believe the one to be his son, and the other a Spanish nobleman, his friend.

This discovery, having thus got vent, was diffused like air; everybody sucked it in, and let it out again with their breath to the next they met withal, and in half an hour's time it was talked of in the house where our adventurers were lodged. Aurelian was stark mad at the news, and knew what search would be immediately made for him. Hippolito, had he not been desperately in love, would certainly have taken horse and ridden out of town just then, for he could make no longer doubt of being discovered, and he was afraid of the just exceptions Leonora might make to a person who had now deceived her twice.

Well, we will leave them both fretting and contriving to no purpose to look about and see what was done at the palace where their doom was determined much quicker than they imagined.

Dinner ended, the Duke retired with some chosen friends to a glass of wine, among whom were the Marquis of Viterbo and Don Fabio. His Highness was no stranger to the long feud that had been between the two families, and also understood what overtures of reconciliation had been lately made with the proposals of marriage between Aurelian and the Marquis' daughter. Having waited till the wine had taken the effect proposed, and the company were raised to an uncommon pitch of cheerfulness, which he also encouraged by an example of freedom and good humour, he took an opportunity of rallying the two grave signors into an accommodation. That was seconded with the praises of the young couple, and the whole company joined in a large encomium upon the graces of Aurelian and the beauties of Juliana. The old fellows were tickled with delight to hear their darlings so admired, which the Duke perceiving, out of a principle of generosity and friendship, urged the present consummation of the marriage, telling them there was yet one day of public rejoicing to come, and how glad he should be to have it improved by so acceptable an alliance, and what an honour it would be to have his cousin's marriage attended by the conjunction of so extraordinary a pair, the performance of which ceremony would crown the joy that was then in agitation, and make the last day vie for equal glory and happiness with the first. In short, by the complaisant and persuasive authority of the Duke, the Dons were wrought into a compliance, and accordingly embraced and shook hands upon the matter.

This news was dispersed like the former, and Don Fabio gave orders for the enquiring out his son's lodging that the Marquis and he might make him a visit as soon as he had acquainted Juliana with his purpose, that she might prepare herself. He found her very cheerful with

Donna Catharina and several other ladies; whereupon the old gentleman, pretty well warmed with the Duke's good fellowship, told her aloud he was come to crown their mirth with another wedding; that His Highness had been pleased to provide a husband for his daughter, and he would have her provide herself to receive him tomorrow. All the company at first, as well as Juliana herself, thought he had rallied, till the Duke, coming in, confirmed the serious part of his discourse. Juliana was confounded at the haste that was imposed on her, and desired a little time to consider what she was about. But the Marquis told her she should have all the rest of her life to consider in; that Aurelian should come and consider with her in the morning if she pleased; but, in the meantime, he advised her to go home and call her maids to counsel.

Juliana took her leave of the company very gravely, as if not much delighted with her father's raillery. Leonora happened to be by and heard all that passed. She was ready to swoon, and found herself seized with a more violent passion than ever for Aurelian. Now, upon her apprehensions of losing him, her active fancy had brought him before her with all the advantages imaginable, and though she had before found great tenderness in her inclination towards him, yet was she somewhat surprised to find she really loved him. She was so uneasy at what she had heard that she thought it convenient to steal out of the presence and retire to her closet to bemoan her unhappy helpless condition.

Our two cavalier-lovers had racked their invention till it was quite disabled, and could not make discovery of one contrivance more for their relief. Both sat silent, each depending upon his friend, and still expecting when the t'other should speak. Night came upon them while they sat thus thoughtless, or rather drowned in thought; but a servant, bringing lights into the room, awakened them, and Hippolito's speech, ushered by a profound sigh, broke silence.

'Well!' said he. 'What must we do, Aurelian?'

'We must suffer,' replied Aurelian, faintly; when, immediately raising his voice, he cried out, 'O ye unequal powers! Why do ye urge us to desire what ye doom us to forbear; give us a will to choose, then curb us with a duty to restrain that choice! Cruel Father, will nothing else suffice! Am I to be the sacrifice to expiate your offences past; past ere I was born? Were I to lose my life, I'd gladly seal your reconcilement with my blood. But, oh my soul is free! You have no title to my immortal being that has existence independent of your power. And must I lose my love, the extract of that being, the joy, light, life, and darling of my soul? No, I'll own my flame, and plead my title too. – But hold, wretched Aurelian, hold, whither does thy passion hurry thee? Alas! the cruel fair Incognita loves thee not! She knows not of thy love! If she did, what merit hast thou to pretend? – Only Love. – Excess of Love. And all the world has that. All that have seen her. Yet I had only seen her once, and in that once I loved above the world; nay, loved beyond myself, such vigorous flame, so strong, so quick she darted at my breast. It must rebound, and by reflection, warm herself. Ah! welcome thought, lovely deluding fancy, hang still upon my soul, let me but think that once she loves, and perish my despair.'

Here a sudden stop gave a period also to Hippolito's expectation, and he hoped, now that his friend had given his passion so free a vent, he might recollect and bethink himself of what was convenient to be done. But Aurelian, as if he had mustered up all his spirits purely to acquit himself of that passionate harangue, stood mute and insensible like an alarum clock that had spent all its force in one violent emotion. Hippolito shook him by the arm to rouse him from his lethargy when his lackey, coming into the room, out of breath, told him there was a coach just stopped at the door, but he did not take time to see who came in it. Aurelian concluded immediately it was his father in quest of him, and without saying any more to Hippolito than that he was ruined if discovered, took his sword and slipped down a back pair of stairs into the garden from whence he conveyed himself into the street.

Hippolito had not bethought himself what to do before he perceived a lady come into the chamber close veiled, and make towards him. At the first appearance of a woman, his imagination flattered him with a thought of Leonora, but that was quickly over upon nearer approach to the lady who had much the advantage in stature of his mistress. He very civilly accosted her, and asked if he were the person to whom the honour of that visit was intended. She said her business was with Don Hippolito di Saviolina, to whom she had matter of concern to import, and which required haste. He had like to have told her that he was the man, but by good chance, reflecting upon his friend's adventure who had taken his name, he made answer that he believed Don Hippolito not far off, and if she had a moment's patience he would enquire for him. He went out, leaving the lady in the room, and made search all round the house and garden for Aurelian, but to no purpose.

The lady, impatient of his long stay, took a pen and ink and some paper which she found upon the table, and had just made an end of her letter when, hearing a noise of more than one coming upstairs, she concluded his friend had found him and that her letter would be to no purpose, so tore it in pieces, which she repented when, turning about, she found her mistake and beheld Don Fabio and the Marquis of Viterbo just entering at the door. She gave a shriek at the surprise of their appearance which much troubled the old gentlemen and made them retire in confusion for putting a gentlewoman into such a fright. The Marquis, thinking they had been misinformed, or had mistaken the lodgings, came forward again and made an apology to the lady for their error. But she, making no reply, walked directly by him downstairs and went into her coach, which hurried her away as speedily as the horses were able to draw.

The Dons were at a loss what to think when Hippolito, coming into the room to give the lady an account of his errand, was no less astonished to find she was departed and had left two old signors in her stead. He knew Don Fabio's face for Aurelian had shown him his father at the tilting, but, being confident he was not known to him, he ventured to ask him concerning a lady whom just now he had left in that chamber. Don Fabio told him she was just gone down, and doubted they had been guilty of a mistake in coming to enquire for a couple of gentlemen whom they were informed were lodged in that house. He begged his pardon if he had any relation to that lady, and desired to know if he could give them any account of the persons they sought for. Hippolito made answer he was a stranger in the place, and only a servant to that lady whom they had disturbed, and whom he must go and seek out. And in this perplexity he left them, going again in search of Aurelian to inform him of what had passed.

The old gentlemen, at last meeting with a servant of the house, were directed to Signor Claudio's chamber, where they were no sooner entered but Aurelian came into the house. A servant, who had skulked for him by Hippolito's order, followed him up into the chamber and told him who was with Claudio then making enquiry for him. He thought that to be no place for him, since Claudio must needs discover all the truth to his father; wherefore he left directions with the servant where Hippolito should meet him in the morning.

As he was going out of the room he espied the torn paper which the lady had thrown upon the floor. The first piece he took up had Incognita written upon it, the sight of which so alarmed him he scarce knew what he was about; but, hearing a noise of a door opening overhead, with as much care as was consistent with the haste he was then in, he gathered up the scattered pieces of paper and betook himself to a ramble.

Coming by a light which hung at the corner of a street, he joined the torn papers and collected thus much: that Incognita had written the note and earnestly desired him (if there were any reality in what he pretended to her) to meet her at twelve o'clock that night at a convent gate. But unluckily the bit of paper which should have mentioned what convent was broken off and lost.

Here was a large subject for Aurelian's passion which he did not spare to pour forth in abundance of curses on his stars. So earnest was he in the contemplation of his misfortunes that he walked on unwittingly, till at length silence – and such as was only to be found in that part of the town whither his unguided steps had carried him – surprised his attention. I say, a profound silence roused him from his thought, and a clap of thunder could have done no more.

Now, because it is possible this, at some time or other, may happen to be read by some malicious or ignorant person (no reflection upon the present reader), who will not admit, or does not understand, that silence should make a man start and have the same effect in provoking his attention with its opposite noise, I will illustrate this matter to such a diminutive critic by a parallel instance of light, which, though it does chiefly entertain the eyes, and is indeed the prime object of the sight, yet should it immediately cease, to have a man left in the dark by a sudden deficiency of it would make him stare with his eyes, and though he could not see, endeavour to look about him. Why, just thus did it fare with our adventurer who, seeming to have wandered both into the dominions of silence and of night, began to have some tender for his own safety, and would willingly have groped his way back again, when he heard a voice, as from a person whose breath had been stopped by some forcible oppression, and, just then, by a violent effort, was broken through the restraint.

'Yet, yet –' again replied the voice, still struggling for air. 'Forbear – and I'll forgive what's past –'

'I have done nothing yet that needs a pardon,' says another, 'and what is to come will admit of none.' Here the person who seemed to be the oppressed made several attempts to speak, but they were only inarticulate sounds, being all interrupted and choked in their passage.

Aurelian was sufficiently astonished, and would have crept nearer to the place whence he guessed the voice to come, but he was got among the ruins of an old monastery, and could not stir so silently but some loose stones he met with made a rumbling. The noise alarmed both parties, and as it gave comfort to the one, it so terrified the other that he could not hinder the oppressed from calling for help. Aurelian fancied it was a woman's voice, and immediately drawing his sword, demanded what was the matter. He was answered with the appearance of a man who had opened a dark lantern[11] which he had by him, and came towards him with a pistol in his hand ready cocked.

Aurelian, seeing the irresistible advantage his adversary had over him, would fain have retired, and, by the greatest providence in the world, going backwards fell down over some loose stones that lay in his way, just in that instant of time when the villain fired his pistol, who, seeing him fall, concluded he had shot him. The cries of the afflicted person were redoubled at the tragic sight, which made the murderer, drawing a poniard, to threaten him that the next murmur should be his last. Aurelian, who was scarce assured that he was unhurt, got softly up, and coming near enough to perceive the violence that was used to stop the injured man's mouth – for now he saw plainly it was a man – cried out: 'Turn, villain, and look upon thy death!'

The fellow, amazed at the voice, turned about to have snatched up the lantern from the ground, either to have given light only to himself or to have put out the candle that he might have made his escape. But which of the two he designed nobody could tell but himself; and if the reader have a curiosity to know, he must blame Aurelian who, thinking there could be no foul play offered to such a villain, ran him immediately through the heart so that he dropped down dead at his feet without speaking a word. He would have seen who the person was he had thus happily delivered, but the dead body had fallen upon the lantern which put out the candle. However, coming up towards him, he asked him how he did and bid him be of good heart. He was answered with nothing but prayers, blessings and thanks, called a thousand deliverers, good geniuses and guardian angels. And the rescued would certainly have gone upon his knees to have worshipped him had he not been bound hand and foot; which Aurelian, understanding, groped for the knots, and either untied them or cut them asunder, but 'tis more probable the latter, because more expeditious.

They took little heed what became of the body which they left behind them, and Aurelian was conducted from out the ruins by the hand of him he had delivered. By a faint light issuing from the just-rising moon, he could discern that it was a youth, but coming into a more frequented part of the town, where several lights were hung out, he was amazed at the extreme beauty which appeared in his face, though a little pale and disordered with his late fright. Aurelian longed to hear the story of so odd an adventure, and entreated his charge to tell it him by the way, but he desired him to forbear till they were come into some house or other where he might rest and recover his tired spirits, for yet he was so faint he was unable to look up. Aurelian thought these last words were delivered in a voice whose accent was not new to him. That thought made him look earnestly in the youth's face which he now was sure he had somewhere seen before, and thereupon asked him if he had never been at Siena. That question made the young gentleman look up, and something of a joy appeared in his countenance, which yet he endeavoured to smother. So praying Aurelian to conduct him to his lodging, he promised him that as soon as they should come thither he would acquaint him with anything he desired to know. Aurelian would rather have gone anywhere else than to his own lodging, but being so very late he was at a loss, and so forced to be contented.

As soon as they were come into his chamber, and that lights were brought them and the servant dismissed, the paleness which so visibly before had usurped the sweet countenance of the afflicted youth vanished and gave place to a more lively flood of crimson, which with a modest heat glowed freshly on his cheeks. Aurelian waited with a pleasing admiration the discovery promised him, when the youth, still struggling with his resolution, with a timorous haste pulled off a peruke which had concealed the most beautiful abundance of hair that ever graced one female head: those dishevelled spreading tresses, as at first they made a discovery of, so at last they served for a veil to the modest lovely blushes of the fair Incognita. For she it was and none other.

But oh! the inexpressible, inconceivable joy and amazement of Aurelian! As soon as he durst venture to think, he concluded it to be all vision, and never doubted so much of anything in his life as of his being then awake. But she, taking him by the hand and desiring him to sit down by her, partly convinced him of the reality of her presence.

'This is the second time, Don Hippolito,' said she to him, 'that I have been here this night. What the occasion was of my seeking you out, and how by miracle you preserved me, would add too much to the surprise I perceive you to be already in should I tell you. Nor will I make any further discovery till I know what censure you pass upon the confidence which I have put in you, and the strange circumstances in which you find me at this time. I am sensible they are such that I shall not blame your severest conjectures, but I hope to convince you when you shall hear what I have to say in justification of my virtue.'

'Justification!' cried Aurelian. 'What infidel dares doubt it!' Then, kneeling down and taking her hand: 'Ah, madam,' says he, 'would Heaven would no other ways look upon than I behold your perfections. – Wrong not your creature with a thought he can be guilty of that horrid impiety as once to doubt your virtue. – Heavens!' cried he, starting up, 'am I so really blessed to see you once again! May I trust my sight? – Or does my fancy now only more strongly work? – For still I did preserve your image in my heart, and you were ever present to my dearest thoughts –'

'Enough, Hippolito, enough of rapture,' said she. 'You cannot much accuse me of ingratitude, for you see I have not been unmindful of you. But moderate your joy till I have told you my condition, and if, for my sake, you are raised to this delight, it is not of a long continuance.'

At that, as Aurelian tells the story, a sigh diffused a mournful sweetness through the air, and liquid grief fell gently from her eyes, triumphant sadness sat upon her brow, and even sorrow seemed delighted with the conquest he had made. See what a change Aurelian felt! His heart bled tears and trembled in his breast. Sighs, struggling for a vent, had choked each other's passage up. His floods of joys were all suppressed; cold doubts and fears had chilled 'em with a sudden frost, and he was troubled to excess – yet knew not why. Well, the learned say it was sympathy, and I am always of the opinion with the learned, if they speak first.

After a world of condolence had passed between them, he prevailed with her to tell him her story. So having put all her sighs into one great sigh, she discharged herself of 'em all at once, and formed the relation you are just about to read.

'Having been in my infancy contracted to a man I could never endure, and now by my parents being likely to be forced to marry him is, in short, the great occasion of my grief. I fancied,' continued she, 'something so generous in your countenance, and uncommon in your behaviour while you were diverting yourself and rallying me with expressions of gallantry at the ball as induced me to hold conference with you. I now freely confess to you, out of design, that if things should happen as I then feared, and as now they are come to pass, I might rely upon your assistance in a matter of concern, and in which I would sooner choose to depend upon a generous stranger than any acquaintance I have. What mirth and freedom I then put on were, I can assure you, far distant from my heart, but I did violence to myself out of complaisance to your temper. – I knew you at the tilting, and wished you might come off as you did; though I do not doubt but you would have had as good success had it been opposite to my inclinations. – Not to detain you by too tedious a relation, every day my friends urged me to the match they had agreed upon for me before I was capable of consenting. At last their importunities grew to that degree that I found I must either consent, which would make me miserable, or be miserable by perpetually enduring to be baited by my father, brother and other relations. I resolved yesterday, on a sudden, to give firm faith to the opinion I had conceived of you, and accordingly came in the evening to request your assistance in delivering me from my tormentors by a safe and private conveyance of me to a monastery about four leagues hence where I have an aunt who would receive me, and is the only relation I have averse to the match. I was surprised at the appearance of some company I did not expect at your lodgings which made me in haste tear a paper which I had written to you with directions where to find me, and get speedily away in my coach to an old servant's house, whom I acquainted with my purpose. By my order she provided me of this habit which I now wear. I ventured to trust myself with her brother, and resolved to go under his conduct to the monastery. He proved to be a villain, and, pretending to take me a short and private way to the place where he was to take up a hackney coach (for that which

I came in was broken somewhere or other with the haste it made to carry me from your lodging), led me into an old ruined monastery, where it pleased Heaven, by what accident I know not, to direct you. I need not tell you how you saved my life and my honour by revenging me with the death of my perfidious guide. This is the sum of my present condition, bating the apprehensions I am in of being taken by some of my relations, and forced to a thing so quite contrary to my inclinations.'

Aurelian was confounded at the relation she had made, and began to fear his own estate to be more desperate than ever he had imagined. He made her a very passionate and eloquent speech on behalf of himself – much better than I intend to insert here – and expressed a mighty concern that she should look upon his ardent affection to be only raillery or gallantry. He was very free of his oaths to confirm the truth of what he pretended, nor I believe did she doubt it, or at least was unwilling so to do; for I would caution the reader, by the by, not to believe every word which she told him, nor that admirable sorrow which she counterfeited to be accurately true. It was indeed truth so cunningly intermingled with fiction that it required no less wit and presence of mind than she was endowed with so to acquit herself on the sudden. She had entrusted herself indeed with a fellow who proved a villain to conduct her to a monastery, but one which was in the town and where she intended only to lie concealed for his sake, as the reader shall understand ere long: for we have another discovery to make to him if he have not found it out of himself already.

After Aurelian had said what he was able upon the subject in hand, with a mournful tone and dejected look, he demanded his doom. She asked him if he would endeavour to convey her to the monastery she had told him of. 'Your commands, madam,' replied he, 'are sacred to me, and were they to lay down my life I would obey them.' With that he would have gone out of the room to have given order for his horses to be got ready immediately, but with a countenance so full of sorrow as moved compassion in the tender-hearted Incognita.

'Stay a little, Don Hippolito,' said she. 'I fear I shall not be able to undergo the fatigue of a journey this night. – Stay, and give me your advice how I shall conceal myself if I continue tomorrow in this town.'

Aurelian could have satisfied her she was not then in a place to avoid discovery – but he must also have told her then the reason of it, viz. whom he was, and who were in quest of him, which he did not think convenient to declare till necessity should urge him, for he feared lest her knowledge of those designs which were in agitation between him and Juliana might deter her more from giving her consent. At last he resolved to try his utmost persuasions to gain her, and told her accordingly he was afraid she would be disturbed there in the morning, and he knew no other way – if she had not as great an aversion for him as the man whom she now endeavoured to avoid – than by making him happy to make herself secure. He demonstrated to her that the disobligation to her parents would be greater by going to a monastery, since it was only to avoid a choice which they had made for her, and which she could not have so just a pretence to do till she had made one for herself.

A world of other arguments he used which she contradicted as long as she was able, or at least willing. At last she told him she would consult her pillow, and in the morning conclude what was fit to be done. He thought it convenient to leave her to her rest, and, having locked her up in his room, went himself to repose upon a pallet by Signor Claudio.

In the meantime, it may be convenient to enquire what became of Hippolito. He had wandered much in pursuit of Aurelian, though Leonora equally took up his thoughts. He was reflecting upon the oddness and extravagance of his circumstances, the continuation of which had doubtless created in him a great uneasiness, when it was interrupted with the noise of opening the gates of the Convent of St Lawrence, whither he was arrived sooner than he thought for, being the place Aurelian had appointed by the lackey to meet him in. He wondered to see the gates opened at so unseasonable an hour, and went to enquire the reason of it from them who were employed. But they proved to be novices, and made him signs to go in, where he might meet with somebody allowed to answer him. He found the religious men all up, and tapers lighting everywhere. At last he followed a friar who was going into the garden, and asking him the cause of these preparations, he was answered that they were entreated to pray for the soul of a cavalier who was just departing or departed this life, and whom, upon further talk with him, he found to be the same Lorenzo so often mentioned.

Don Mario, it seems, uncle to Lorenzo and father to Leonora, had a private door out of the garden belonging to his house into that of the convent, which door this father was now a-going to open that he and his family might come and offer up their orisons for the soul of their kinsman. Hippolito, having informed himself of as much as he could ask without suspicion, took his leave of the friar, not a little joyful at the hopes he had by such unexpected means of seeing his beautiful Leonora. As soon as he was got at convenient distance from the friar (who 'tis like, he thought, had returned into the convent to his devotion), he turned back through a close walk which led him with a little compass to the same private door where just before he had left the friar, who now he saw was gone, and the door open.

He went into Don Mario's garden, and walked round with much caution and circumspection, for the moon was then about to rise, and had already diffused a glimmering light sufficient to distinguish a man from a tree. By computation now (which is a very remarkable circumstance) Hippolito entered this garden near upon the same instant when Aurelian wandered into the old monastery and found his Incognita in distress. He was pretty well acquainted with the platform and sight of the garden, for he had formerly surveyed the outside, and knew what part to make to if he should be surprised and driven to a precipitate escape. He took his stand behind a well-grown bush of myrtle which, should the moon shine brighter than was required, had the advantage to be shaded by the indulgent boughs of an ancient bay tree. He was delighted with the choice he had made for he found a hollow in the myrtle, as if purposely contrived for the reception of one person who might, undiscovered, perceive all about him. He looked upon it as a good omen that the tree consecrated to Venus was so propitious to him in his amorous distress. The consideration of that, together with the obligation he lay under to the Muses for sheltering him also with so large a crown of bays, had like to have set him a-rhyming.

He was, to tell the truth, naturally addicted to madrigal, and we should undoubtedly have had a small desert of numbers to have picked and criticised upon had he not been interrupted just upon his delivery, nay, after the preliminary sigh had made way for his utterance. But so was his fortune, Don Mario was coming towards the door at that very nick of time where he met with a priest just out of breath who told him that Lorenzo was just breathing his last, and desired to know if he would come and take his final leave before they were to administer the extreme unction. Don Mario, who had been at some difference with his nephew, now thought it his duty to be reconciled to him. So, calling to Leonora who was coming after him, he bid her go to her devotions in the chapel, and told her where he was going.

He went on with the priest while Hippolito saw Leonora come forward, only accompanied by her woman. She was in an undress, and by reason of a melancholy visible in her face, more careless than usual in her attire, which he thought added as much as was possible to the abundance of her charms. He had not much time to contemplate this beauteous vision, for she soon passed into the garden of the convent, leaving him confounded with love, admiration, joy, hope, fear, and all the train of passions which seize upon men in his condition all at once. He was so teased with this variety of torment that he never missed the two hours that had slipped away during his automacy and intestine conflict. Leonora's return settled his spirits, at least united them, and he had now no other thought but how he should present himself before her, when she, calling her woman, bid her bolt the garden door on the inside that she might not be surprised by her father if he returned through the convent; which done, she ordered her to bring down her lute and leave her to herself in the garden.

All this Hippolito saw and heard to his inexpressible content, yet had he much to do to smother his joy and hinder it from taking a vent which would have ruined the only opportunity of his life. Leonora withdrew into an arbour so near him that he could distinctly hear her if she played or sung. Having tuned her lute, with a voice soft as the breath of angels, she sung to it this following air:

Ah! whither, whither shall I fly,
A poor unhappy maid:
To hopeless love and misery
By my own heart betrayed?
Not by Alexis' eyes undone,
Nor by his charming faithless tongue,
Or any practised art:
Such real ills may hope a cure,
But the sad pains which I endure
Proceed from fancied smart.

'Twas fancy gave Alexis charms,
Ere I beheld his face:
Kind fancy (then) could fold our arms,

And form a soft embrace.
But since I've seen the real swain,
And tried to fancy him again,
I'm by my fancy taught,
Though 'tis a bliss no tongue can tell,
To have Alexis; yet 'tis hell
To have him but in thought.

The song ended grieved Hippolito that it was so soon ended, and in the ecstasy he was then rapt, I believe he would have been satisfied to have expired with it. He could not help flattering himself – though at the same time he checked his own vanity – that he was the person meant in the song. While he was indulging which thought, to his happy astonishment he heard it encouraged by these words:

'Unhappy Leonora,' said she, 'how is thy poor unwary heart misled? Whither am I come? The false deluding lights of an imaginary flame have led me, a poor benighted victim, to a real fire. I burn and am consumed with hopeless love; those beams in whose soft temperate warmth I wantoned heretofore, now flash destruction to my soul; my treacherous greedy eyes have sucked the glaring light; they have united all its rays, and, like a burning-glass[12], conveyed the pointed meteor to my heart. – Ah! Aurelian, how quickly hast thou conquered, and how quickly must thou forsake. Oh happy – to me, unfortunately happy – Juliana! I am to be the subject of thy triumph. To thee, Aurelian, comes laden with the tribute of my heart, and glories in the oblation of his broken vows. – What then, is Aurelian false? False! Alas, I know not what I say. How can he be false, or true, or anything to me? What promises did he ere make or I receive? Sure I dream, or I am mad, and fancy it to be love. Foolish girl! recall thy banished reason. – Ah! would it were no more, would I could rave, sure that would give me ease and rob me of the sense of pain. At least among my wandering thoughts I should at sometime light upon Aurelian, and fancy him to be mine. Kind madness would flatter my poor feeble wishes and sometimes tell me Aurelian is not lost – not irrecoverably – not for ever lost.'

Hippolito could hear no more; he had not room for half his transport. When Leonora perceived a man coming towards her, she fell a-trembling and could not speak. Hippolito approached with reverence, as to a sacred shrine. When coming near enough to see her consternation, he fell upon his knees.

'Behold, O adored Leonora,' said he, 'your ravished Aurelian! Behold at your feet the happiest of men! Be not disturbed at my appearance, but think that Heaven conducted me to hear my bliss pronounced by that dear mouth alone whose breath could fill me with new life.'

Here he would have come nearer, but Leonora (scarce come to herself) was getting up in haste to have gone away. He caught her hand, and with all the endearments of love and transport pressed her stay. She was a long time in great confusion. At last, with many blushes, she entreated him to let her go where she might hide her guilty head and not expose her shame before his eyes, since his ears had been sufficient witnesses of her crime. He begged pardon for his treachery in overhearing, and confessed it to be a crime he had now repeated. With a thousand submissions, entreaties, prayers, praises, blessings, and passionate expressions he wrought upon her to stay and hear him.

Here Hippolito made use of his rhetoric, and it proved prevailing: 'twere tedious to tell the many ingenious arguments he used, with all her nice distinctions and objections. In short, he convinced her of his passion, represented to her the necessity they were under of being speedy in their resolves: that his father (for still he was Aurelian) would undoubtedly find him in the morning, and then it would be too late to repent. She, on the other hand, knew it was in vain to deny a passion which he had heard her so frankly own (and no doubt was very glad it was past and done). Besides apprehending the danger of delay, and having some little jealousies and fears of what effect might be produced between the commands of his father and the beauties of Juliana, after some decent denials she consented to be conducted by him through the garden into the convent where she would prevail with her confessor to marry them. He was a scrupulous old father whom they had to deal withal, insomuch that ere they had persuaded him, Don Mario was returned by the way of his own house, where, missing his daughter, and her woman not being able to give any further account of her than that she left her in the garden, he concluded she was gone again to her devotions, and indeed he found her in the chapel upon her knees, with Hippolito in her hand, receiving the father's benediction upon conclusion of the ceremony.

It would have asked a very skilful hand to have depicted to the life the faces of those three persons at Don Mario's appearance. He that has seen some admirable piece of transmutation by a gorgon's head may form to himself the most probable idea of the prototype. The old gentleman was himself in a sort of a wood to find his daughter with a young fellow and a priest, but as yet he did not know the worst, till Hippolito and Leonora came, and, kneeling at his feet, begged his forgiveness and blessing as his son and daughter. Don Mario, instead of that, fell into a most violent passion, and would undoubtedly have committed some extravagant action had he not been restrained, more by the sanctity of the place than the persuasions of all the religious who were now come about him. Leonora stirred not off her knees all this time, but continued begging of him that he would hear her.

'Ah! Ungrateful and undutiful wretch!' cried he. 'How hast thou requited all my care and tenderness of thee? Now, when I might have expected some return of comfort, to throw thyself away upon an unknown person and, for ought I know, a villain. To me I'm sure he is a villain, who has robbed me of my treasure, my darling joy, and all the future happiness of my life prevented. Go – go, thou now-to-be-forgotten Leonora! Go and enjoy thy unprosperous choice. You, who wanted not a father's counsel, cannot need, or else will slight, his blessing.'

These last words were spoken with so much passion and feeling concern that Leonora, moved with excess of grief, fainted at his feet, just as she had caught hold to embrace his knees. The old man would have shook her off, but compassion and fatherly affection came upon him in the midst of his resolve and melted him into tears. He embraced his daughter in his arms and wept over her while they endeavoured to restore her senses.

Hippolito was in such concern he could not speak, but was busily employed in rubbing and chafing her temples, when she, opening her eyes, laid hold of his arm and cried out, 'Oh my Aurelian! How unhappy have you made me!' With that she had again like to have fainted away, but he took her in his arms, and begged Don Mario to have some pity on his daughter, since by his severity she was reduced to that condition. The old man, hearing his daughter name Aurelian, was a little revived, and began to hope things were in a pretty good condition. He was persuaded to comfort her, and having brought her wholly to herself, was content to hear her excuse, and in a little time was so far wrought upon as to beg Hippolito's pardon for the ill opinion he had conceived of him, and not long after gave his consent.

The night was spent in this conflict, and it was now clear day when Don Mario, conducting his new son and daughter through the garden, was met by some servants of the Marquis of Viterbo who had been enquiring for Donna Leonora to know if Juliana had lately been with her; for that she was missing from her father's house and no conjectures could be made of what might become of her. Don Mario and Leonora were surprised at the news, for he knew well enough of the match that was designed for Juliana, and having enquired where the Marquis was, it was told him that he was gone with Don Fabio and Fabritio towards Aurelian's lodgings. Don Mario, having assured the servants that Juliana had not been there, dismissed them and advised with his son and daughter how they should undeceive the Marquis and Don Fabio in their expectations of Aurelian. Hippolito could oftentimes scarce forbear smiling at the old man's contrivances who was most deceived himself. He at length advised them to go all down together to his lodging, where he would present himself before his father and ingenuously confess to him the truth, and he did not question his approving of his choice.

This was agreed to, and the coach made ready. While they were upon their way, Hippolito prayed heartily that his friend Aurelian might be at the lodging to satisfy Don Mario and Leonora of his circumstances and quality when he should be obliged to discover himself. His petitions were granted, for Don Fabio had beset the house long before his son was up or Incognita awake.

Upon the arrival of Don Mario and Hippolito they heard a great noise and hubbub above stairs, which Don Mario concluded was occasioned by their not finding Aurelian, whom he thought he could give the best account of: so that it was not in Hippolito's power to dissuade him from going up before to prepare his father to receive and forgive him. While Hippolito and Leonora were left in the coach at the door, he made himself known to her, and begged her pardon a thousand times for continuing the deceit. She was under some concern at first to find she was still mistaken, but his behaviour and the reasons he gave soon reconciled him to her; his person was altogether as agreeable, his estate and quality not at all inferior to Aurelian's.

In the meantime, the true Aurelian, who had seen his father, begged leave of him to withdraw for a moment, in which time he went into the chamber where his Incognita was dressing herself, by his design, in woman's apparel. While he was consulting with her how they should break the matter to his father, it happened that Don Mario came upstairs where the Marquis and Don Fabio were. They undoubtedly concluded him mad to hear him making apologies and excuses for Aurelian, whom he told them, if they would promise to forgive, he would present before them immediately. The Marquis asked him if his daughter had lain with Leonora that night; he answered him with another question on behalf of Aurelian. In short, they could not understand one another, but each thought the other beside himself. Don Mario was so concerned that they would not believe him that he ran downstairs and came to the door out of breath, desiring Hippolito that he would come into the house quickly, for that he could not persuade his father but that he had already seen and spoken to him.

Hippolito, by that, understood that Aurelian was in the house. So, taking Leonora by the hand, he followed Don Mario, who led him up into the dining room where they found Aurelian upon his knees, begging his father to forgive him that he could not agree to the choice he had made for him since he had already disposed of himself, and that before he understood the designs he had for him, which was the reason that he had hitherto concealed himself. Don Fabio knew not how to answer him, but looked upon the Marquis, and the Marquis upon him, as if the cement had been cooled which was to have united their families. All was silent, and Don Mario for his part took it to be all conjuration. He was coming forward to present Hippolito to them when Aurelian, spying his friend, started from his knees and ran to embrace him.

'My dear Hippolito,' said he, 'what happy chance has brought you hither, just at my necessity?' Hippolito pointed to Don Mario and Leonora, and told him upon what terms he came. Don Mario was ready to run mad hearing him called Hippolito, and went again to examine his daughter. While she was informing him of the truth, the Marquis' servants returned with the melancholy news that his daughter was nowhere to be found. While the Marquis and Don Fabritio were wondering at and lamenting the misfortune of her loss, Hippolito came towards Don Fabio and interceded for his son, since the lady perhaps had withdrawn herself out of an aversion to the match. Don Fabio, though very much incensed, yet forgot not the respect due to Hippolito's quality, and by his persuasion spoke to Aurelian, though with a stern look and angry voice, and asked him where he had disposed the cause of his disobedience, if he were worthy to see her or no. Aurelian made answer that he desired no more than for him to see her, and he did not doubt a consequence of his approbation and forgiveness.

'Well,' said Don Fabio, 'you are very conceited of your own discretion. Let us see this rarity.'

While Aurelian was gone in for Incognita, the Marquis of Viterbo and Don Fabritio were taking their leaves in great disorder for their loss and disappointment, but Don Fabio entreated their stay a moment longer till the return of his son. Aurelian led Incognita into the room veiled, who, seeing some company there which he had not told her of, would have gone back again. But Don Fabio came bluntly forward, and ere she was aware, lifted up her veil and beheld the fair Incognita, differing nothing from Juliana but in her name.

This discovery was so extremely surprising and welcome that either joy or amazement had tied up the tongues of the whole company. Aurelian here was most at a loss for he knew not of his happiness and that which all along prevented Juliana's confessing her self to him was her knowing Hippolito (for whom she took him) to be Aurelian's friend, and she feared if he had known her that he would never have consented to have deprived him of her. Juliana was the first that spoke, falling upon her knees to her father, who was not enough himself to take her up. Don Fabio ran to her, and awakened the Marquis, who then embraced her, but could not yet speak. Fabritio and Leonora strove who should first take her in their arms; for Aurelian he was out of his wits for joy, and Juliana was not much behind him, to see how happily their loves and duties were reconciled. Don Fabio embraced his son and forgave him. The Marquis and Fabritio gave Juliana into his hands; he received the blessing upon his knees. All were overjoyed, and Don Mario not a little proud at the discovery of his son-in-law, whom Aurelian did not fail to set forth with all the ardent zeal and eloquence of friendship. Juliana and Leonora had pleasant discourse about their unknown and mistaken rivalship, and it was the subject of a great deal of mirth to hear Juliana relate the several contrivances which she had to avoid Aurelian for the sake of Hippolito.

Having diverted themselves with many remarks upon the pleasing surprise, they all thought it proper to attend upon the Great Duke that morning at the palace, and to acquaint him with the novelty of what had passed; while, by the way, the two young couples entertained the company with the relation of several particulars of their three days' adventures.

NOTES

1. The Levesons and the Congreves were both old Staffordshire families.
2. Cleophil was the pseudonym Congreve adopted in his early writing career.
3. Minerva is the Roman goddess of wisdom.
4. 'Our minds are not so moved by what we are told / As by what's brought before our very eyes / And we see for ourselves.' (Horace, *The Art of Poetry*, ll. 180–2; translated by J.G. Nichols)
5. The three dramatic rules, as derived from Aristotle and Horace, were the unity of time, the unity of place, and the unity of action.
6. The Medicean fortress of Poggio Imperiale is situated in the town of Poggibonsi, just south of Florence; it was formerly the residence of the grand dukes of Tuscany.
7. A joust.
8. Porter (from the Italian *facchino*).
9. The Greek philosopher Epicurus (*c.* 341–271 BC) believed in the existence of only atoms and void.
10. Credit.
11. A lantern with a sliding panel in order to conceal its light.
12. A lens that focuses the sun's rays in such a way that they fall on a very small space which is ignited as a result; burning-glasses were used as an early means of ignition.

BIOGRAPHICAL NOTE

William Congreve was born near Leeds in 1670. His father, a soldier, was posted to Youghal soon after Congreve's birth, and as a result Congreve spent his childhood in Ireland. He was educated at Kilkenny, where he befriended Jonathan Swift, and the two of them progressed to Trinity College, Dublin. He went on to study at the Middle Temple, but soon gave up law in favour of pursuing a career in literature; to which end he served his apprenticeship under the tutelage of John Dryden, the foremost playwright of the day.

His first novel, *Incognita* (1692), was published under the name of 'Cleophil', and it was not until the success of his comedy *The Old Bachelor* in 1693 that Congreve was recognised as a writer. *The Double Dealer* (1693) and *Love for Love* (1695) appeared soon after this, followed, in 1697, by his only tragedy, *The Mourning Bride*. His last – and most famous – dramatic work was *The Way of the World* (1700) whose ingenious story of a pair of lovers and their unconventional marriage has come to be regarded as one of the greatest comedies in the English language.

Congreve produced no more plays after 1700, perhaps partly due to the cool reception given to *The Way of the World*, and partly to his failing health; he suffered from gout and poor eyesight. His literary output was instead confined to writing librettos. He also became involved in politics, holding various minor positions, and he enjoyed the friendships of Swift, Pope, Voltaire, and the Duchess of Marlborough who allegedly bore him an illegitimate daughter.

Congreve died on 19th January 1729, the result of a carriage accident as he was travelling to Bath. He is buried in Westminster Abbey.

HESPERUS PRESS – 100 PAGES

Hesperus Press, as suggested by the Latin motto, is committed to bringing near what is far – far both in space and time. Works written by the greatest authors, and unjustly neglected or simply little known in the English-speaking world, are made accessible through new translations and a completely fresh editorial approach. Through these short classic works, each around 100 pages in length, the reader will be introduced to the greatest writers from all times and all cultures.

For more information on Hesperus Press, please visit our website: **www.hesperuspress.com**

ET REMOTISSIMA PROPE

SELECTED TITLES FROM HESPERUS PRESS

Author	*Title*	*Foreword writer*
Pietro Aretino	*The School of Whoredom*	Paul Bailey
Jane Austen	*Love and Friendship*	Fay Weldon
Honoré de Balzac	*Colonel Chabert*	A.N. Wilson
Charles Baudelaire	*On Wine and Hashish*	Margaret Drabble
Giovanni Boccaccio	*Life of Dante*	A.N. Wilson
Charlotte Brontë	*The Green Dwarf*	Libby Purves
Mikhail Bulgakov	*The Fatal Eggs*	Doris Lessing
Giacomo Casanova	*The Duel*	Tim Parks
Miguel de Cervantes	*The Dialogue of the Dogs*	
Anton Chekhov	*The Story of a Nobody*	Louis de Bernières
Wilkie Collins	*Who Killed Zebedee?*	Martin Jarvis
Arthur Conan Doyle	*The Tragedy of the Korosko*	Tony Robinson
Joseph Conrad	*Heart of Darkness*	A.N. Wilson
Gabriele D'Annunzio	*The Book of the Virgins*	Tim Parks
Dante Alighieri	*New Life*	Louis de Bernières
Daniel Defoe	*The King of Pirates*	Peter Ackroyd
Marquis de Sade	*Incest*	Janet Street-Porter
Charles Dickens	*The Haunted House*	Peter Ackroyd
Fyodor Dostoevsky	*Poor People*	Charlotte Hobson
Joseph von Eichendorff	*Life of a Good-for-nothing*	
George Eliot	*Amos Barton*	Matthew Sweet
F. Scott Fitzgerald	*The Rich Boy*	John Updike
Gustave Flaubert	*Memoirs of a Madman*	Germaine Greer
E.M. Forster	*Arctic Summer*	Anita Desai
Ugo Foscolo	*Last Letters of Jacopo Ortis*	Valerio Massimo Manfredi
Elizabeth Gaskell	*Lois the Witch*	Jenny Uglow
Théophile Gautier	*The Jinx*	Gilbert Adair

André Gide	*Theseus*	
Nikolai Gogol	*The Squabble*	Patrick McCabe
Thomas Hardy	*Fellow-Townsmen*	Emma Tennant
Nathaniel Hawthorne	*Rappaccini's Daughter*	Simon Schama
E.T.A. Hoffmann	*Mademoiselle de Scudéri*	Gilbert Adair
Victor Hugo	*The Last Day of a Condemned Man*	Libby Purves
Joris-Karl Huysmans	*With the Flow*	Simon Callow
Henry James	*In the Cage*	Libby Purves
Franz Kafka	*Metamorphosis*	Martin Jarvis
Heinrich von Kleist	*The Marquise of O–*	Andrew Miller
D.H. Lawrence	*The Fox*	Doris Lessing
Leonardo da Vinci	*Prophecies*	Eraldo Affinati
Giacomo Leopardi	*Thoughts*	Edoardo Albinati
Nikolai Leskov	*Lady Macbeth of Mtsensk*	Gilbert Adair
Niccolò Machiavelli	*Life of Castruccio Castracani*	Richard Overy
Katherine Mansfield	*In a German Pension*	Linda Grant
Guy de Maupassant	*Butterball*	Germaine Greer
Herman Melville	*The Enchanted Isles*	Margaret Drabble
Francis Petrarch	*My Secret Book*	Germaine Greer
Luigi Pirandello	*Loveless Love*	
Edgar Allan Poe	*Eureka*	Sir Patrick Moore
Alexander Pope	*Scriblerus*	Peter Ackroyd
Alexander Pushkin	*Dubrovsky*	Patrick Neate
François Rabelais	*Gargantua*	Paul Bailey
François Rabelais	*Pantagruel*	Paul Bailey
Friedrich von Schiller	*The Ghost-seer*	Martin Jarvis
Percy Bysshe Shelley	*Zastrozzi*	Germaine Greer
Stendhal	*Memoirs of an Egotist*	Doris Lessing
Robert Louis Stevenson	*Dr Jekyll and Mr Hyde*	Helen Dunmore

Theodor Storm	*The Lake of the Bees*	Alan Sillitoe
Italo Svevo	*A Perfect Hoax*	Tim Parks
Jonathan Swift	*Directions to Servants*	Colm Tóibín
W.M. Thackeray	*Rebecca and Rowena*	Matthew Sweet
Leo Tolstoy	*Hadji Murat*	Colm Tóibín
Ivan Turgenev	*Faust*	Simon Callow
Mark Twain	*The Diary of Adam and Eve*	John Updike
Giovanni Verga	*Life in the Country*	Paul Bailey
Jules Verne	*A Fantasy of Dr Ox*	Gilbert Adair
Edith Wharton	*The Touchstone*	Salley Vickers
Oscar Wilde	*The Portrait of Mr W.H.*	Peter Ackroyd
Virginia Woolf	*Carlyle's House and Other Sketches*	Doris Lessing
Virginia Woolf	*Monday or Tuesday*	Scarlett Thomas
Emile Zola	*For a Night of Love*	A.N. Wilson